THE SHIVERING GROUND

& other stories

sara barkat

T. S. Poetry Press • New York

T. S. Poetry Press
Briarcliff, New York
Tspoetry.com

Cover painting by Edward Degas. Retouched by rawpixel.
https://www.flickr.com/photos/vintage_illustration/

Art, in order of appearance:

"Early printed parchment leaf, probably from a missal" by Provenance Online Project (public domain).

"Plongeon imbrin ailes" photographed by Johann Dréo (CC BY-SA 1.0). https://creativecommons.org/licenses/by-sa/1.0/legalcode

Plate 332 of Birds of America depicting Pied duck (now known as Labrador duck) illustrated by John James Audobon (public domain).

"Depiction from 'Jottings during the cruise of H.M.S. Curacoa among the South Sea Island's in 1865 by Julius L. Brenchley." Illustrated by Joseph Smit (public domain).

"Spectacled Cormorant, Pallas' Cormorant" illustrated by Joseph Wolf (public domain).

"Live male in Whitman's aviary" from "Bird Lore" photograph by the Audobon Society (public domain).

"Live captive Carolina Parakeet" photographed by Robert Wilson Shufeldt (public domain).

ISBN 978-1-943120-54-3

Cataloging-in-Publication Data:
Barkat, Sara
[Fiction. Science Fiction. Eco-Fiction.]
The Shivering Ground & Other Stories./Sara Barkat
ISBN 978-1-943120-54-3

Contents

✷

The Door at the End of the Path

The door had been there ever since Shelley could remember. In the back of the walled garden, the path leading through brambles to come upon it, suddenly—first sunflowers in tilted rows, the tumble of stones and dirt turned over, spiderwebs strewn with dew; then, behind the brambles, past the pachysandra and ferns, up it came: the wall, and the doorway in red crumbling brick, and ivy. It had no keyhole, as a door should; nothing to peek through and wonder about: it had no knob at all—indeed, if it were not for the fact that it was, very clearly, a door; set within a frame, still with its weathered wood, splintered and greyed by years, it would not have seemed very much like a door at all. There was no indentation; no marks where a handle might once have been, and Shelley had spent long enough pulling her hands along the grasses by the wall's end, poking amidst the dirt with sticks and pointed rocks. She would have found a handle, if it had fallen off or been thrown there; the way she had found the pottery, the broken bottles of glass, blue and green and brown, and put them in a pile in the old stone bird-feeder that was never filled with anything but a thin skim of muddy water and, in the autumn, a drift of leaves. Sometimes, she would lean her head very close to the ground as though maybe she could peer *under* the door, but it was flush with the brick, and the scree of dirt across it was never disturbed by as much as a runnel of water coming through.

So impenetrable was this door that it became the indefatigable imaginative resource: anything could be behind it, and sometimes was. On peaceful, sunny afternoons, she could hear the hooves of horses going by, and imagine lords and ladies dressed in their fine clothes as though in a mediaeval Romance; on grey, sullen days the washing on the line flapped as women bustled quickly out, glancing toward the sky, putting everything into baskets as fast as they could before those first, cold, unforgiving drops of rain.

Shelley had tapped on the door, too, and sometimes in the winter when the snowdrifts fell with great shuddering crackles, she could almost fancy that another little girl, quite like her, tapped back from the other side.

No one else saw the purpose of the door; for they did not venture so far into the wilds of the back garden, near the wall, in the corners. Perhaps, in truth, the most mundane possible explanations existed: but even those had their thrill. Another house, near their own, had once wanted a doorway from yard to yard, but after a feud had sawn off the handles; an artist with a flair for the mysterious had commissioned a false door to be built just for the occasion, never intending it to be opened at all.

In the mornings Shelley had her tutors and in the afternoons she played, but in the evening she sat with her family in the long, crooked dining room on the ground floor. It was a most peculiar room, and I am sure that most people would agree not a singularly pleasant one. For, long ago, it had been a hallway connecting the kitchen to other rooms in the house; and when the other walls had been knocked aside to create a photography studio of the rest of the floor, the hallway had been neglected: and so it was that it became a dining room.

The great wooden table fairly scraped the walls on either

side, and to climb onto the small chairs with their seats that smelled like old fabric Shelley had to duck under the table and shimmy up on the other side: while her mother sat on one end, where the door to the photography studio was; and her father on the other, where lay the door to the kitchen and the front hall and the stairwell. And on each of the walls, which were papered with the most peculiar old paper in innumerable zebraesque stripes, were the photographs her mother took.

It was art, and many people paid highly for it, and sometimes if Shelley was very good and very quiet she could stand in the corners of the room and watch the lights being positioned and the sets propped up and the customers with their tall buttoned coats. But though there was always an air of mysterious business in the studio itself, the photographs were strange things, and certainly did not help the atmosphere of mashed peas.

Lying at odd angles amid pools of blackness were the skins of animals with staring eyes, and upon it in varying states ranging from fancy dress to artfully-placed sheets were the figures, which sat or contorted themselves with the oddest countenances, as though they were being statues. Some, in fact, looked almost lifeless; and one particular young woman, with long, winding hair, lay on what seemed to be the side of a cliff-fall with her hair about her neck. In monochrome it looked strangely like blood, or a rope; her palms, opened below her, were like pieces that had been cut off, coming from the bones of animals in a huge and solemn pile on either side.

"Did your studies go well today?" Mother would ask, and Shelley would tell her about Geography and History and the maps she had traced with her fingers, wondering about that so-vast world beyond, and the ships and engines that could take one there.

"Did you find anything new in the garden?" Father would ask, and Shelley would tell him about the new species of butterfly that had alighted on the milkweed, or the precise route of the ants from their sandy home near where the hose connected to the wall with a spinning wheel like a pirate's ship.

Neither of them asked about the door in the wall, and if Shelley mentioned it, and what had been happening beyond it that day, they would say, "That's very nice, dear," and that would be all.

When the plates had been cleared off Shelley would be sent up to her room again, and would read, or play with the strange carven animals her mother had made. But they looked very much like the photographs, and so when Shelley was done playing she would put them back in their shelves, facing the walls, so that nothing could look at her when she slept: and a very sensible precaution she thought it was, too.

Now there was one particular model who came to the house on occasion, and he had a false eye which he'd chosen to get in a different color, to be more inspiring: it was like a lion's eye, and he would sometimes take it out to scare Shelley. But Shelley, who found it much less intimidating than the pictures in the hall, would only nod politely and agree that it was indeed a ghastly sight.

This particular model never was as brusque or as harried as the others, and did not carry a watch. "What time is it, dear lady," he would always ask Mother, who would know quite off the top of her head; and when he went to be posed they always spent some time walking this way and that before the lights were adjusted, with Mother showing him just how he ought to look this time, and tilting his face as she pleased, while his one real eye watched her, and his cane, which he had put down by the door, watched Shelley with its bird-shaped head.

Funny thing, isn't it? the bird-head might ask occasionally. *No one else seems to need so many pictures taken as that man.*

Oh, well, Shelley might reply, *I'm sure he must be famous and rich; and he is obviously quite vain of his appearance—though it is a bit grotesque when he takes out his eye.*

But the bird-head always cackled at Shelley's careful answers, as though it knew something that she had not said, and that *it* would never say. And Shelley would give it a terrible glare, and, if it persisted in its sly expression, would hood it with the piece of cloth used to stop up reflections.

Father, of course, went out to work; and in the morning he was always very busy. Sometimes, after breakfast, Shelley would watch him run about fifteen times from his room to the washroom and back again, as he found things he had forgotten and added other papers to his ever-growing stack. Father's work, Shelley found, was much harder to understand than Mother's. All she knew was that it encompassed Figures, and that many people were always making Predictions. She wondered how it was that though anyone could make Predictions, and they could even be accurate Predictions, the only ones paid for it were those who had framed pieces of paper to account for it.

"Have a good day, seashell," he would say before he left, while Shelley held his hat and peered out onto the street, which was always filled with dust and unaccountably loud as soon as Father opened the door. Then, taking his hat and shoving it onto his head, he would rush out into the mass of busy people and all at once look nothing at all like Father anymore: in fact, if it were not for the particular way his hat had been squished ever since one of her wooden animals sat on it, Shelley would hardly have been able to tell his brown-coated figure from anyone else's.

One afternoon, when Shelley had just finished her walk around the garden, nodding, at last, to the door in the wall and pressing her fingers against the wood, tugging on vines, she came in to find that the kitchen door was blocked by buckets and booted feet, and recalled that there had been something with pipes that needed fixing. She was quite shy of the workmen, and so instead of walking through the kitchen she sneaked around the house to the side door. Taking off her muddy boots outside she slipped into the photography studio, muffling the bell on the door with one hand so as not to cause an interruption.

Shelley could tell right away from the bird-head cane by the door that the famous gentleman must be about, and she walked ever so quiet past the strange, unfathomable shapes of stands and things that cluttered up the corners of the large room. The empty, tattered wood floor beneath her was very soft and helped her along without creaking a bit. On the other side of the room was the door to the hallway, and once she got there, she could open it a crack and be up to her room to change into something appropriate for evening wear.

The lights were pointed inward toward the modeling space, and a grand table was set up covered in fine foods, as in some of Mother's Greek themes. The man with the glass eye was holding a bunch of grapes in his hand, and Shelley thought to herself that it didn't look at all like the right prop for him: they were so round and dark and fragile they made him seem quite intimidating and piratical; while with something else he might have come across as full of mournful hauteur. He picked one of the grapes between his fingers, which caught the bright lights like a bloody circle, and held it out to Mother, who leaned forward with her teeth and bit down right in the middle. It popped, and the juice went flying; and Shelley felt something that was neither revulsion nor dismay, but quite so overpowering that she felt all of a sudden overcome with the need to hide. But at that moment, as though springing out in answer, the trembling rack of false swords by her hand caught her finger and fell with a deafening clatter to the floor.

Mother and the famous gentleman sprang up as though startled, and Mother called out, carefully, "Shelley… dear? Is that you?"

But Shelley had found a very smart place to hide; in a false-coffin, and when Mother and the man with the false eye went tromping past, they saw only the pile of swords lying on the ground.

"Hmm," Mother said, and that was all; then she bent to place them all back.

It was late when Shelley made it to the dining room that day, and when she looked down the hall to Mother and Father, the photographs seemed especially strange: for one, in the corner, was tilted as though it were about to jump!

"Mother," Shelley said, when she had talked about her studies and the wonders of the garden, "why do you never put pictures of the man with the glass eye on the wall with the rest?"

There was a silence that seemed, if anything, vaster than the usual silence; and then with a careful *click* of silverware Mother put down her fork.

"Not everyone is capable of becoming Art," she said carefully.

Father picked up his glass of wine and stared into it. "A man with a glass eye, did you say, seashell?" he asked. "What does he look like?"

"Well he—" Shelley said, and jumped when Mother stood up very quickly.

"This isn't the place nor the time," she said.

"It never quite is," Father said mildly. But he stood up too, and without saying another word Mother and Father both left, Mother through her door and Father through his, and all at once Shelley was sitting in the center of a long, empty table, right in the middle of dinner, by herself.

She waited, because she didn't want to be scolded if Mother and Father came back to find her having gotten up without being excused, but they didn't come back very soon. She could hear the rumbling of the workmen's steps in the kitchen, and other steps going up to the floor above, and she built a tower of her silverware: and then, finally, she became bored and uncomfortable enough to get up regardless.

Without even bothering to put on her boots—for she had no wish to creep through the photography studio again—she slipped quickly through the kitchen, past the things being opened and the smell of something rotten in the pipes, which was stronger here than anywhere in the house. The workmen were all standing around and exclaiming in odd tones, and the lines of their backs stood up like fence-posts. At the kitchen door Shelley slipped out in only her stockings, and ran out into the garden, feeling a terrible, uncomfortable itch; she felt that she had done something wrong, but did not know what, and only knew she could not stay still. And the only place Shelley could think of to go was to her door, which always seemed to have a story behind it.

But when she got to the back of the garden, there, where the door had always been, was only a gaping, empty spot, with a mailbox nailed to it. And on the other side of a very discreet fence went zooming past all the cars and bicycles and carriages along the street, moving faster and faster like the ants by the water hose, as though they were afraid!

✵

Conditions

The old black and white film skipped past stage lightning and the monstrous, black-lined eyes opened in a pale, staring face—"it's alive!" Dr. Stein flipped to another channel. It was a dark night. He had the lamp on, but the pale glow of the TV was engaged in an eerie battle with the incandescent bulb. It was a stormy night too, and the wind had been rattling the windows like zombies trying the latch; thunder shook the house and drowned out the small lifeless cheer of the movies. He was alone in the house, in the wake of his sister's visit.

There was no one Dr. Stein hated more than his sister. In looks, the siblings were alike enough to be twins, and this made his mouth twist unpleasantly. It was distasteful to him. They were both high-cheekboned and sallow, with dark, somber eyes and straight brown hair. His eyelashes were long, her chin was square.

The argument had raged up and down the house for hours. It was the usual questions: "So what have you been doing lately?" He worked at a science facility, top secret. He told her anyway.

"We've come close to creating artificial life; think of it—we can become God."

His sister laughed. Her laugh was grating, too sure of itself, and it made him feel weak. His sister was a lawyer. She dressed in black suits that made her look powerful, and she always wore heels.

"Haven't you learned already? The creation always kills the creator. That's what we did with God."

Dr. Stein smiled thinly. They were in his study, and his sister walked by the dark bookshelves, tracing her fingers across wood that wasn't expensive but built as though it was. She took the titles out to flip through, then put them back in the wrong place, upside-down.

"Re-animation of corpses," Dr. Stein murmured to himself.

He had jump cables in his basement. The car was in the garage but the battery had been removed and brought downstairs. He had wires connected to his lightning rod. Energy could not be created or destroyed, just passed from one thing to the next, the only common inheritance. In the dim light, he had rats floating in jars; he caught them in traps and preserved them so that when he walked down the steps with a flashlight he could look into their staring eyes. Electricity could create movement in death. Perhaps it had the energy of life, perhaps the static he felt touching the TV screen was the remains of those life-forces, gathering, trying to pass into him.

When they sat down in the small kitchen with its checkered grey and pink formica it was as if the memory of all those family dinners came and sat beside them. They ate macaroni and cheese from a box. Dr. Stein hated it. He kept a collection of those boxes in the pantry, for when his sister came to visit. She hated it more. She picked carefully through the garish orange liquid and ate with undisguised disgust. She talked about the last case she had won, defending a man accused of murder.

"Was he innocent?" Dr. Stein asked, watching a fly buzz itself around the light and not swatting it, because his sister flinched at the static crack when its wings moved.

"No," she said, and swallowed gingerly.

"Do you ever wonder if he'll murder someone else?" Dr.

Stein said, with a vague curiosity, not of care for whoever might be killed or from a sense of justice, but to learn his sister's answer.

"I don't."

"It could be you."

"It wouldn't be," she said, lining up her fork and knife to convey her displeasure. "I saved his life."

"A man could hate someone for that," Dr. Stein said.

His sister threw the fork down with a clatter.

"That was years ago, Archie—and if you think I would have stood aside while my little brother tried to commit suicide you have another thing coming." She stood up, turned on the tap so it ran enough to steam, and washed the dishes with quick fury.

"I wasn't talking about that," he said, and watched the fly.

"Weren't you?" Her voice was subdued, and almost disappeared in the insubstantial whir of the heater turning on automatically. The wind was picking up.

The fly took another turn around the room and came in reach of the table; Dr. Stein picked up his empty cup and turned it over on the fly. It darted from side to side hitting the glass.

"Why do you torture the poor creature?" his sister said, turning around. Her arms were crossed, and in the light from the bare bulb with the dark and empty windows behind her, she looked severe, like an image in an old movie.

"I'll let it out, if you like," Dr. Stein said. He tapped the side of the glass where the fly had alighted, and stared at its small, black body and its vibrating wings. His sister didn't answer.

The raccoon had died once, on his back porch, the garbage can overturned and everything scattered over the concrete. He left the garbage where it was, and took the body to the basement. It was still there now, preserved and sitting on the metal table.

The shine was harsh and unpleasant as he connected the wires, waiting for a crack of lightning. No monster yet, but when the creature blinked its eyes and the connecting monitor showed the sudden spike of a heartbeat his breath froze in his throat in the excitement of the moment.

The beast was wild, possessed of an inarticulate fury and intent to kill that drove it to dive from the table in attack, but leaving the electric connection it faltered, stumbled on its feet in dull confusion and died again.

Outside, the wind was growing louder—now the trees beyond the window, like mourners, bent beneath the fury of the storm, and against the window, tracks of rain spilled sideways like lead. Dr. Stein walked to the window and pushed it up, old wood creaking and water blowing in onto his skin, cold. The darkness held only shadows but still he stared into it. He leaned his head out further, gripping tightly to the sill and pulling in. When he closed the window, the sudden barrier was jarring; he ran his fingers through his wet hair once and watched the rainbow sides of droplets falling.

~

Down the basement steps, all seventeen, the black outline of her legs blocked the light from above as she stepped down, stairs creaking gently in warning.

"Don't you keep any lights on down here?" she called, one hand still on the rail.

"I have a light on." The blue glow of the directed lamp shone above the polished metal as Dr. Stein emptied a rat from a jar and hooked it up to wires. A shock, and another, and he watched the small thing blink at him in sleepy confusion.

"I managed to get rid of the aggression effect but now the animals are too passive," he observed. "They have no sense of self-preservation." He brought the blowtorch close and saw the smoke and burning rise from its flesh as it watched him, until once again the heartbeat stopped. Internal organs couldn't keep it up. There was a soft smile curling the edge of his mouth and he looked away as his sister walked over to him. She stood beyond the glow of the lamp, and only the gleam of her eyes could be seen.

"It's past midnight," she said.

"The best time to create life," he answered.

She laughed shortly, and he dumped the body in the waste disposal can and closed the lid.

Past midnight, and the rain stopped, leaving a cool breeze and hints of rustling leaves. Whatever language the night spoke was incomprehensible to him. They walked up the old wooden steps, smoothed but splintering under their feet, and the lone bulb hummed in the kitchen, where blue shadows mixed with yellow and rain lay on the steps past the crack in the screen door. It glittered like pale diamonds.

"Do you want the heat?" Dr. Stein asked, watching the shape of her white hand clenched against the rail. She let go, and the rail remained.

"No, it's fine," his sister said, and he turned from the thermostat. The round face behind plastic was still and inorganic, desperately so. With the last hint of thunder, so went the life, and he felt awkward.

His sister strode out past the kitchen, and into the living room with its stained beige carpet and the red couch. She sat on the edge, crossing her legs; her heels through the glass surface of the coffee table looked pulled from ink.

"They named galvanism after the man who created it," she said. "He ran electricity through frogs' legs, and watched them jump. But he hadn't found life, only sparks moving through flesh."

Dr. Stein turned off the kitchen light, and in the suddenness of the dark, shadows were, without having done anything but appear. The refrigerator hummed its lonely vibrations, bumping through the space where the light had been, and he went to the living room, sitting on a deep stuffed chair beyond her silhouette.

"You never have any good movies," she said, flipping through the stack beside the couch, the plastic covers of the disc cases shining out wan and flickering beams toward the wall.

"Do you believe in souls?" he asked.

"I never said that."

"There's no reason to believe life can't be electrically reproduced, if all the variables are accounted for," he said. "It might take decades, but it's not impossible."

"That rat on the table moved, but it no longer acted with a will. How do you know it was still the same rat that had died? If even one of the variables changed, who's to say what you created had anything in common with what it had been? Its memories, its past—were those gone too?"

"Does it matter if it was the same rat?"

She put the movies down on the table. She twined her fingers, each manicured nail sharp and distinct, and her breath was slow, with an almost imperceptible hesitation.

"I don't know."

Sometimes, when he was alone and evening had overstayed its welcome he would take off his shirt in front of the bathroom mirror and stare at his reflection–the skinny frame, the scars—and wonder if he had died that day. It was a familiar fantasy, playing out like a worn reel of film, the true details distorted and fuzzed, the image projected on a screen. If he had—and that was the question; if they had not arrived in time, would she have walked a careful circle around his body, her heels making pockmarks of blood on the wooden floor? He disregarded the fact that his sister had never worn heels till college.

He would imagine that she cut apart his body, replacing his heart with machinery, his blood with gasoline, and wound a twisting key through his center until he jerked and shuddered to life. The problem remained that he was different, and belonged to her. He thought, sometimes, that it might have happened this way.

"I knew a man named David," his sister said. Dr. Stein pushed his finger into the hole in the chair where the stuffing came out and pulled, lightly. Like cotton candy, or some new kind of cloud, it spooled itself from the old patterned fabric, a sickly xanthic shade.

"Was he a lawyer too?"

"He sang."

Dr. Stein tried to imagine his sister going—where? To a crowded bar somewhere, tired after work; or no, an opera;—passing a man on the street with his hat out for crumpled bills. He watched the way his sister's hands tightened spasmodically around each other, and her eyes, looking down, were lost under the black line of her lashes. "We were involved," she said. "For two years."

"What happened to him?" he asked. He knew something must have happened. She would never have mentioned him otherwise.

"He was…odd," she replied. "We had an apartment together,

you know, and one night I came back to find the windows open, the electricity off, but there was a swarm of lightning bugs covering the walls. Their wings, opening and shutting, made the whole house look alive; like it was the flank of an animal, breathing; the room was lit yellow-green like a spotlight from all sides. A few of them flew around him in clockwise spirals, blinking like they were speaking in code. I was by the door, I couldn't walk inside. He asked me what was wrong and I said it was him. He came over to the door, held out his hand, and led me in. We danced until the dark started to steal away and the fireflies with it, and I closed every window and locked the door. It never happened again." She looked up at her brother and leaned back.

Dr. Stein pulled the stuffing from one hand to another and looked away. "He sounds like my kind of person," he said at last.

"He wasn't," his sister replied. "Everyone liked him."

Dr. Stein smiled.

"He said he'd come to the country to observe—to see the sights before they all disappeared, you know. The ones in the guidebook. It was always dog-eared, the amount of times he paged through, checking off one place after another in charcoal and pencil and ink. It always seemed so morbid, those bright photographs two-dimensionalizing space. I asked him, once, why he noticed me. I had never been to any of those places, until he came; I didn't care to."

"What did he say?" Dr. Stein asked.

"He said I was like one of those moths in the larval stage, mummified in amber for millions of years. He said it amused him to see if I would ever crawl my way out. I told him that creatures like that are better off staying where they are. If they emerge, it will be to a world in which the only possibilities are their own death, from lack of natural habitat and predation, or the opposite—their overrunning a world ill-equipped to handle them, and which they will ravage and destroy."

"Are you predicting the moth apocalypse?" Dr. Stein said.

"Yes," his sister said, dryly. "It's a good thing we turned out all the lights."

"If the power went out, we wouldn't know," he said. It had been such a storm, it could have happened. He couldn't help imagining lightning striking a tree, the wind blowing down wires weighed under the burden of branches, the wet roads, cars on the curb and anxious groups gathered around the live current. Too much electricity did strange things to the human organism, reset those electromagnetic paths within the brain, stopped the heart, turned ordinary men into musicians. A lightning strike might bring the dead back to life.

"The refrigerator is still running," his sister said. "I can hear it."

She had better ears than him.

In the morning of the next day, after his sister had left, Dr. Stein stood on the front porch next to the puddles lying brown and muddy over the gravel drive. The air was still and quiet, the leaves that remained were like green and dripping umbrellas. He could smell petrichor, and the uncontrollable growing things that sprang from the dark earth. Maples tried to insinuate themselves into his driveway, the small grassy stalks with two bud-like leaves, bright and soft, their roots already clinging to the dirt. Beyond the bend of the drive, the main road could not be seen, only heard; the traffic a constant irritant, the man-made equivalent to that other impossibility, the waterfall—both had that same mundane sound. He imagined that the ground might have split overnight, that a river sprang up and all the cars were buried under the rush of water. He got into his own vehicle, then cranked his windows down as he drove to work, turned off the radio, daring a sudden blockage. There was a crash along one road that slowed everything to a crawl, but he got through, flashing his badge at the guards who had known him for six years, they waved him into the complex. The computer labs were buzzing, the generators droned and clattered outside.

"The power didn't go out where you were?" his coworker said, his suit jacket off, his polished shoes squeaking on the floor.

"No," Dr. Stein replied. "Is it out in many places?"

"All over the county," the man said. "You're a lucky bastard."

The technicians added links in the neural network, dumped in data, waited for the AI to respond. It looked uncannily lifelike, from the waist up; sitting behind that table as if they were reporting to it. He always walked the other way, behind the thing's back, so he could see the mess of wires and glinting microchips. He wondered if that disturbed it, if it was capable of feeling the same uncanny itch down its spine as a human with their back unprotected.

This wasn't his division, this pure mechanical device. His own lab created chimeras, strange combinations of the biological and the inorganic, cyborgs in the making. Perhaps someday it would be impossible to tell the electric sheep from the living ones, until they were autopsied.

The previous night's conversation returned to him. She had asked, "Do you remember the last fall?"

"Of course I do," he answered, while the imperceptible hum of the refrigerator, in the next room, proved that there was still life beyond this moment. In that same year, tsunamis up the coast had destroyed the rest of those cities he'd only heard about, and the TV was an always-uncomfortable static. All the wreckage, all the ruin, and the ground was brilliant red. Every morning, he would wake to more of the world ending, and the earth laid out a scarlet cloak as though waiting for an emperor to arrive.

Nothing doing. He'd killed ants on the back porch, pulled apart their legs, their antennae, trying to see how they moved. One or two had wings. He'd dreamed of the soft orange of a honeybee, lost in that sticky gestalt. They had found honey in the pyramids, buried among the dead—in case they'd gotten hungry on their journey. He wondered what the dead did now, without any more paths to guide them to the stars.

"He just disappeared one day," she said at last. "Something had been brewing for weeks, but I ignored it. There was a case taking up all my attention."

"I understand," Dr. Stein said. His sister shook her head.

"He'd been trying to talk to me. He left this by our bed." She reached into her purse, pulled out a slim, soft-cover book. In colorful, childlike lines, a fair-haired boy on a rock stared out into endless space.

"The Little Prince," he said, taking it from her.

"Yes." Her voice was hard, and he couldn't tell if her tone held recrimination, or merely disinterest.

"You think it was a suicide note?"

"Maybe," she said. "Maybe not. He might have just left—gone to find the next thing on his list. He took the guidebook with him—it wasn't even halfway filled out."

"And when it is," Dr. Stein said, "do you think he'll come back?"

"No," she said. "He was done with me, and I was done with him long before that."

"Then why the concern? Why mention it at all?"

"I wondered what your opinion might be."

"They say that bodies are too heavy to bring along with you," Dr. Stein said, flipping through the book, looking at the tiny, careful letters; the planets, each small enough for only one idea—except for this one. Here, you had to wait to see the sunset.

"Is that what you were trying to do?"

Dr. Stein smiled. He imagined it looked stretched–thin, inhuman.

"No," he said. "I was just trying to die."

She frowned at him, as though unconvinced, but she turned on the TV. An old movie was playing—static-lined and grey.

"Happy birthday, Archie," she said, standing up, pulling her phone out–the thin square of light unfolded, then went dark. She brought her purse close to her body with one hand as she put it back. "You can keep the book."

He stood up, too. "Are you leaving? In this storm?"

"The storm is over," she said. She smiled, slightly, almost sadly; and something in it flickered. "The time for magic is done." She kissed him, gently, on the cheek, and went out to check her car. Through the front screen, he could see her dark figure bent against it, hear the beep of the key unlocking, the lights turning on. She may have looked his way at last—the glare of the headlights rendered her dark and unreadable. Then she got in and turned on the gas.

He stepped out, when the last glow and the sound of the engine had vanished into the trees, and looked up into the sky above him. In the blackness of the outage, the usually-empty space was strewn with a wild abundance of glowing pearls, uncalculably far; the light reached down, touching his skin like silk, then fading away.

✳

The Eternal In-Between

You fell asleep one evening like any other, and there were summer insects making soft music, chime-chime, peep-peep, in a way that had a kind of repetition to it and an aliveness. This comforted you, the thing about aliveness, because you'd been having too much of the opposite recently. Outside where the cars rattled you could imagine the doctors in their oilskins and canes tapping past, hooked beaks glinting, and leaving behind in the air the scent of lavender. But you hadn't been out much, recently. Everything that was necessary could be brought by the windows on the small hot air balloons blazoned with company logos, dropping pizza in a cardboard box end over end in a hilarious slow-motion *tumble* until the tray at the balcony caught it, and that was it: technology was grand. No more need for touch, and a good thing too, because with the ships earlier in the year had come the death, with its buboes and rats and fleas, and the news would do nothing but blare images of deathbeds and worried faces of those who hid away in the city behind their pan-aluminum embankments and everyone else fled, and a few stayed and buried the bodies.

You didn't want to be here, and that's why sleep felt kind to you, because it was a free no-ticket-required show somewhere else, without all this; you turned down the gas-lamp in the hall and thought about writing to your mother. What would you even say? *Doing fine. Have enough supplies to last out the year. Sanity less.* But there it was: you lived with what you had, and when you hated it, you made new places to live in your mind. You'd been hollowing out the back of an old well for the past week but decided on a whim this evening to let your mind dreamsling itself wherever it wanted; maybe you'd end up somewhere terrifying and dark but at least it wouldn't be boring.

Still the only thing you didn't expect was that round mixing bowl and the hand that held it. *That hand* you'd never seen for years. Left with the last train into the dark forest, where no radio signal could penetrate. Of course your friend had never returned, but neither of you had expected them to anyway.

"Hey," you said, aimlessly. You looked out the window in a shifting brick wall and saw sunlight as bright as an egg yolk and it seemed to drip down the very pane of glass with a burning brilliance, and you wondered if you stuck your hand out into it would you be whirled away, whisked into a meringue?

"You appear well," your friend replied, looking you over, noticing the new boots. Didn't mention the patched up cloak or the way your ungloved hands were almost skeletal, to a degree that disturbed you. You didn't think they could be telling the truth but they had never been one for polite small talk, so you disregarded your reflection in the glass of the bowl they held, and the way your face itself was distorted with the mouth hovering two centimetres off where it should have been. Your friend probably didn't take into account things like that; as long as you had the right number of limbs and a steady heartbeat they were convinced you showed all the signs of being a healthy human being.

"How is it over there?" you said, stepping forward to sit at the counter, pouring flour into the mixture in the bowl, which had begun like clear water but spun darker and darker with each revolution, until it was a black as complete as the night sky with sugar crystals and specks of flour and it looked like stars and further galaxies you might fall into if you got too close; a steadying hand pulled you back.

"Making a new place?" you said.

"Mm-hm," your friend replied. "The old dreams are all withering gray, I don't know why. Perhaps it's because the yew tree is dead."

You felt a pang of discomfort at the pronouncement, a kind of shiver as though the church bells had tolled but it was silent. "Tell me you're still alive," you pleaded, but your friend only shook their head and wouldn't reply. "It needs raisins," they said, at last. You handed it to them in silence. A few rolled out. They were soft and ran together even before they touched the spoon, becoming nothing more than a lump, the skins peeling away. Inside the bowl, an emptiness was rising.

You knew that soon enough you'd wake up, of course, and because none of the carrier pigeons would travel into the forest, and the radio waves were blocked by the dark standing trees with their frowning limbs, towering over the last-minute architecture of the city, this would be the last time you spoke. You wanted to say something about the raisins. Something like, "Why are they crawling like that, why do they have so many wings and flies inside?" but you were already too disturbed by the buzzing shapes. Instead you stopped the endless motion of the spoon, taking your friend's hand.

"Look, there's something I wanted to tell you, before you left," you said. Your words seemed so thin, suddenly, when the spoon was not hurrying its way around, stirring endlessly, clacking against the side. "I wanted to tell you how much I enjoyed riding our bicycles down the vertical street, even though we crashed at the bottom. I wanted to tell you that when we sat there tangled up and I laughed, and I saw something in one of your open eyes, I knew what it meant; and I kept it with me all this time. You see, I have it within me still," you said, and opened your pocket and pulled out a piece of sheet music, the black calligraphy in its careful, blocky dots making the whole thing look like paving stones on a log road. The calligraphy went on and on, and you pulled the entire song out from your skin where you'd kept it, just in case your friend wanted to see it again. But they were already looking down into the bowl. Not one of their hands even touched the brittle parchment, and at last you sat there clutching all these reams of paper in front of a galaxy and laughed a little, from the absurdity of it: because your friend, who had always created worlds like that, so simply, needed one tiny song from a soon-dead person so little.

You thought, in fact, that your friend would in some sense continue on forever because of those galaxies, and perhaps because of some peculiarity in their character not applicable to ordinary men, for your friend had always been in some sense ageless. When you, as a child, walked up the steps to the small whitewashed room, your friend had been sitting on a branch outside the window, bedecked in rings; and when you had toiled long hours in the darkness welding pipes you had seen them beyond every flashing spark, like an afterimage. Still, they had left to go to the forest and had never told you why, and left behind only a half-finished poem as though the clue would tell you everything you needed to know. It didn't. It only went something like "love is not all" and then turned into a list of the periodic table of the elements, and you tried to figure out whether it was the stable or unstable ones; but it was split evenly down the middle.

And for a moment you wondered if you were angry: you should be angry, you thought, because the water you had played in that had been so blue as a child was covered in silt and piles of strange items, like shipwrecks of trash, and in and among them were the corpses of the mermaids that had once sung you to sleep. Perhaps you should be angry, because your friend had never said anything about the way their feet turned backward more and more every time, had only stared out and laughing had listened to your small and fragile stories.

It had been left to you to notice that the wild cloak of brightness that your friend wore, which had once been burnished and shining like golden silk, had somehow turned into an old winter coat with the tags clipped off, and their innumerable hands had always fit into two mittens, and by the time they left for the forest from which no one had ever returned you hardly recognized the creature that stepped away from you, so ordinary did it seem. Like anyone else you had known from childhood, with the same look of bewildered apathy behind their glasses and a cap pulled low over their eyes.

You thought you ought to say something recriminatory about how someone who had always been so much better than you could have done something, changed something, maybe had a duty to stay as unknowable as they had always been, and not fade into oblivion, but that felt both clumsy and untrue. You knew anyhow that it had been half your own fault; for at some point you'd stopped following your friend into the secret places behind the brambles to peer with curious wonder at the spiders' webs, bedecked with their pearled dewdrops and shimmering among the green.

At last you said only, "Will I ever recognize you when you return?"

"I didn't leave," your friend said, and you shook your head.

"Yes you did," you said. "Don't you remember?"

Don't you remember lying on your deathbed while I, myself, wrote the story about the train track and then burnt it in incensed smoke? How could you not recall the way the defeat of the men who turned their heads away with squares over their eyes mocked the fact that you had stepped out the open door? Don't you remember the shape of the road leading into the forest?

You remembered. You remembered and you said it all, while your friend picked up the bowl again, and began to mix. You peered into the bowl of stars, disquieted.

"I don't blame you," your friend continued, "I just worry about the dream that went grey in my hands yesterday, when I bent to pick up a snail on its way through my garden, because I had been so enthralled by the pattern on its shell."

"I'm sorry," you said, and tried to remember if you had ever seen a snail. You thought you had. In a clip-art one time. Maybe. Oh yes: one time, very small, it had hidden under the brown earth near your feet, when you had curled up in a corner, away from the sirens that went through, and the shattering glass from the ships flying low in the sky like old mirrors; putting your hands to your ears while the noise, wailing, got louder and louder: and you had stared at the bright curve of it, a fingernail; a complete and fragile world.

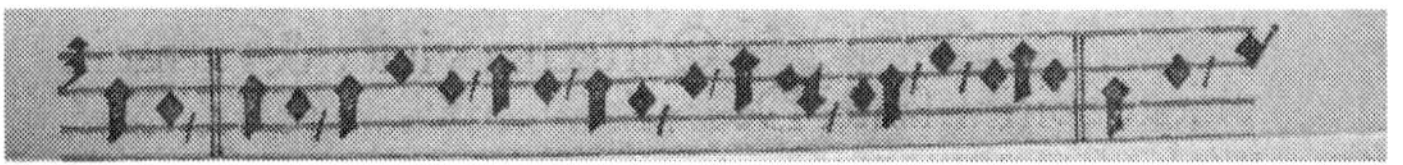

The Mannequin

The mannequin with my heart in it stands in the corner, dusty. It has been that way for years. In the early days I would try futilely to tidy up round it, and when the feathers on the duster, my thin appendage, dragged across that cold aluminum collarbone and the plume of dust leapt up in answer, it would hover, bombinating, susurrating, droning...nothing but flecks of dust, thin-sharded and shining, mica and talc. I got tired of that dust, and the way the windowpane beyond it reeked of grime, and the way I never had to stand on tiptoe or crouch—the mannequin with its knobbed spine and the crooked jaunty tilt of its ear, circles upon circles of insets swirled within brass was always exactly my height. It did not have my hair. It did not, really, have even my shape, but its eyes were like mine, only flat and as completely lifeless as anything can give impression of being.

If it had seemed more alive, perhaps it wouldn't have been so unnerving. Perhaps if, when I put my fingers splayed across its bare chest, I could feel an answering hum within the confines, a sort of bent pull from my heart toward the body that owned it, I would have felt more reassured. As it was there was only solid emptiness, a great, yawning, mechanical absence, and the mannequin soon became nothing more than another *thing* to take up space: a lump, an absent curiosity.

I had been fifteen when the world became unbearable. It had nothing to do with the parabolic retinues of the Order, it had nothing to do with the executions in the square, on the way home from school: I kept my head down like everyone who had any sense and played with the charm bracelet around my wrist. Snowdrop, lily, amaranth—all things I had vaguely heard of, and which still lived a shadowed half-life in my memory, in the neuronal sparking of my brain: microfiche leeching color from the plants, silver washing away the rest in the mass-produced charms. But even though I had high-minded ideals about originality, my own included, I loved the little bracelet, and the worn-smooth petals. *Swip-swip;* my thumb would make smooth tracks on an unchanging surface, and in concert, the pavement below my feet would spin away beyond. Feet all crowded into boots, into sandals, into striped socks, into colored tie-dyed appliquéd, beaded, faux-leather, plastic, buttons, shoelaces, ribbons… that's all I noticed, the ground. I suppose there were others that looked up, and they could tell you a different story about that time.

The real cruelty of life was my self-focused delirium. I had written notes in the corner of my schoolbooks in pencil and the more crowded those notes became the more I could read, as if in a dizzyingly mocking mirror, the vacillation of my own thoughts, oddly spliced together with The Truth; that is, the printed type it sat between. Together, like a pea-plant, it grew new meaning. I became more and more convinced that I was if not a genius, I was at least a visionary, seeing through the incomprehensible nonsense that was spat out for us into some higher purpose. But there was no audience for my prophetic intent.

In more mundane words, I cried every night and missed my best friend, who had Gone Away, at some point. Everyone's had that. There was nothing unique about my sorrow. Somehow, even in the depths of my melodramatic despair, I think I recognized the fact.

It became a problem, at some point, and so my case was referred. For a while we were all standing in stuck horror with the summons through our throats, as though wondering if it were even possible to run. It might have been a medical disaster, only a friend of my teacher's who had seen one of my more unguarded essays recommended that my problem wasn't precisely lack of patriotic spirit, but merely an excess of vision. So I got offered a position in government soon after school.

Why am I telling you this? I know it has nothing to do with my heart. It's context; it explains why everything happened the way it did. These extraneous details are the most important part of any truly thoughtful exercise…

I was twenty-six when, through a referral, I came across the service. It was wildly expensive, but then, I had a comfortable amount of money, and enough trouble sleeping to want the latest palliative. They said it was stress pain, something sunk into the body, something to do with work. I didn't care. What was the building like? Oh, clean… very ordinary. You've seen doctors' offices like it. A discreet address on High Street that no one would ever suspect of such a thing. Or, at least, say in anything other than anti-patriotic jokes repeated under one's breath. They showed me the mannequin. I found nothing wrong with it.

All those other details about the form—everything I've just told you—I only noticed those later. Over time, the buildup of almost imperceptible sensory experiences layered one on top of another finally created a clear enough picture of unease that it made me… uncomfortable. Perhaps the posing helped; the great spotlights, the sterile no-nonsense orderliness within which the mannequin fit perfectly. Sometimes I've seriously considered redecorating my office in tune with the memory of that show-strip just to make the mannequin's presence ubiquitous; I haven't because of the nagging thought that it might somehow gain another aspect—become as unfitting in its glamourous surroundings as it is in the detritus where it now perches.

I was under anesthesia for the actual surgery, of course: you can't just remove someone's heart with only topical medicine. So I can't tell you much about that. But there it is: I had it out, and I felt unaccountably light for quite some time. It was almost easy to forget that it still existed, somewhere, and that it always would for as long as I lived, and that it would exist still—a husk made in my image—long after my death.

One day I found my old journals again—or what I had called my journals—and with the passage of time I was able to see my naïveté for what it was. I think I had them shredded. An embarrassment for me, a potential loss of my job if the wrong people found out about the inclinations of my younger self—I can't imagine why I wasn't ordered to destroy those things years ago. Well, there's always something that slips through the cracks of even the most well-oiled machine, as they say, and the Great Progress is no exception to the matter.

They give you a small key, for emergencies, so you can open up the chest-panel. At first I did so out of pure curiosity, to watch the beating grotesque housing itself in my false flesh. I felt a pure sort of relief that it was no longer in me; it was so slimy and red. Yes, I'm sure I touched it once or twice. Still, over the years… I think it just slipped my mind.

A week ago, you know, when you first spoke to me, I thought about the mannequin, consciously, for the first time in years. I went up to its unworn face and stared into its eyes, and bent my cupped hand, to turn the key in the lock and look at my heart. I don't know why I felt such a sudden urge. I knew it was working smoothly; I was still alive after all, and I'd never showed signs of palpitations or faintness. I think I just wanted a visual reminder; something that showed me movement, that showed me evidence of my own existence.

I put the key in, and…I couldn't turn it. I couldn't open it at all. The lock was rusted shut.

Yes, I know I should have oiled it more. That's not the point. I don't know what the point is. You just asked me 'what's it like' and 'if I recommend the procedure.' Of course I recommend it. It's quite standard and safe. You can ask anyone, they'll tell you the same thing. Many good citizens have done it, many people you know, I'm sure.

All the same, you are my daughter, and I thought that you at least deserved the details—

Of course it changes nothing.

Yes, you'll have a lot more job options open to you if you do.

I love you too.

[beep beep beep beep beep…]

Click.

✳

Brianna

Roses in hints of dusky pink climb the turrets, a blush of soft red like faded blood, some deepening into that shadow, others only the barest hint of coral like the reflection of sunrise in pure clouds. Still, below their trembling small flower, each thorn is sharp and precise. There is no malice in it. A rose is merely a rose. But they know their tempting nature, know how easily such soft petals can bruise. And so they carry swords.

Each leaf is a jagged imprint. The breath of wind rustles the entwined bower. Every prince before has been strangled and pierced, and he knows the dangers. But he has dreamed, dreams of a sleeping maiden waiting inside the constricted spell.

And the roses fall back before his hands, as though heeding his footsteps. And with each heady step he takes he realizes he is not being cast out, and the path between them becomes crushed with the fragrance of petals, laying themselves before his feet. He hears a voice, sees a glimmer, in the reflections of the broken pavement; in that untouched air he feels an indrawn breath.

He climbs to her bed, leans down, and presses one trembling kiss to her lips, and she wakes.

"Oh, my prince," she says, with a soft smile. "I knew you'd find me."

He can feel her smile lighting an answering one of his own, and their fingers reach for each other as though trying to hold tightly in a shaking world. If all went as it should, the flowers would be falling, the spell broken. But there is still such a deathly hush to the place, and he realizes that she is not saved. She is not getting out.

"I'm sorry," she says, quietly, into the crook of his arm. "I'm sorry. I was so selfish. So lonely. I needed someone with me, I kept searching…for someone to answer. And you…" Her hand hovers at the skin of his wrists and the palms of his hands, scratched by thorns. "You've braved much just to join me in solitude."

"With you," he says, "it is not solitude. Don't you think I would have turned back, if I meant to? I don't regret it—not any of it—"

"Shh," she answers, pressing one finger to his mouth, and crying. "Shh. Not yet. But you will someday, you will wish you had left me when you had the chance."

"No," he says, calm and certain. "I won't."

The light turns on. "Peter! What the hell are you doing in there! Oh my god…"

"We were just talking! Bri was scared and we wanted to—"

He's dragged out by one shoulder into the hall. His toes scuff uneasily at the carpet while he hears his parents talking to Bri. "Are you all right?"

He peeks in through the door. Bri's hunched over, the way she does when she gets worried, and hugging her stuffed rabbit. One hand is pulling fretfully at its ear. "Please don't get mad," she says, all at once, quietly. "It was dark and… it was dark and I… I just I…" her eyes close and her hands make fists. She's not looking at anyone anymore. "I'm sorry, I'm sorry,"

"Brianna, you didn't do anything wrong. We're not mad at you, honey. It's just… it's not appropriate to be with Peter at night. Okay? Do you understand?"

Some time later, Bri nods, sniffling. When his parents leave the room he's already crawled back to his own bedroom and pulled the covers over his head as though maybe they'll think he's asleep. It doesn't work.

"Peter."

They're not half so doting as they are to Brianna.

"That was wrong. You know why that was wrong, right?"

"I *told* you we were just talking, I don't *understand* what's wrong. Bri doesn't like it here, she says the house makes noises at night and she says at the orphanage there was always someone nearby…"

They sigh. "Peter, we understand you were just trying to help. But you can't do this, or we're going to have to have her stay at another home. Do you understand?"

Peter freezes. Finally, at last, he nods. His heart is in his throat, and he feels like if he speaks at all, he will scream—and if he screams, Bri is gone forever.

At last he manages a shaking, "Yes. Yes, I understand."

The door closes behind them. And he lies awake thinking about Bri crying in her own bed. And what is he supposed to say? That since the first time they saw each other, they *knew?* A memory that was more than a memory… it had ended in tragedy once, and he knows that he is incapable of fighting fate. Even as a hero.

As a child, he can do less. He curses whatever it was that told his parents where they were. He feels sick, knowing that he's never been able to do anything more for Bri than be with her in her misery, and now not even that.

The first few years are beautiful. The eternal afternoon light that filters through the stone under the gabled roof makes patterns on the dusty floor, and they chase circles through corridors that have long since become mausoleums. At each cavernous hall she has another story: "Here is where my mother used to host the circle of her confidantes, and of the fine dresses they would wear, shimmering jewels and perfumes, it was like being in a painting.... Here my father would sit in state, and the dour ambassadors would glower down at their scrolls.... My brothers would cheat at swordcraft, throwing sand in each other's eyes and wrestling in the mud, if ever their tutors stepped away for even a moment..."

Now each place holds only silence. Still, her voice is almost enough to call those ghostly images forth, as she spins around and swings her careless hands.

It is never dark. But it isn't possible for anyone to stay awake forever.

In that same everlasting afternoon, when the hours wear down, and she has pinched her arms red and bruised and can no longer stay awake, they fall asleep in whatever random corner they've found. Never in her bed. Never in *that room*. And every time, she is terrified.

"What if I don't wake up," she says, her voice a shaking whisper, a rising hiss. "What if you're not here when I do. What if I'm alone again."

"You're not alone," he says.

And he holds her in his arms and feels the rapid-fire pulse of her heart against his, and kisses her chastely while he tries to ignore the terror in her eyes. What can he do for her but be there, when her hands grip his own and her tears stain the brocade of his tunic? What can he ever do to make things right?

The castle has doors, and every one of them is stopped up

with roses. The scent, powerful and cloying, follows him into his dreams.

Peter knows metalcraft still, though swordmaking is an art no longer. Instead, he works on old airship engines at the corner shop. It's a calming act, knowing he's putting something back into the sky, honing it into something that it's meant to be. Bri follows him when she can. "What are you working on today?" he'll ask, sometimes.

"Weapons manifests," she'll answer. Sometimes, rarely, a spark will enter her eyes when she does. "Thirty million new z-guns, parts from the hinterlands. A new stock of plutonium was found."

"That's good, yeah?" Peter will say.

And Bri will laugh. "As good as it gets." But her voice is cynical. He wishes, desperately, that he could remember the sound of her voice when she still knew innocence; that he had thought to fold it in his pocket with the mementos of another life.

"We'll get away from all this soon enough," Peter promises. He flashes her a smile he hopes is convincing; and if it fails, she will not call him on it. "Just a few more years…an airship of our own…"

"And we'll be off," Bri will say. "Just floating above the clouds, far away from all of it…" she'll lean toward him and he'll catch her lazy tilt before she can sprawl across greasy rivets and spoil her blue dress, and she'll smirk at him lazily.

"Come with me…just give it all up…steal a ship and we can leave now."

"You're an ass. And such criminal tendencies you have, Bri. If I didn't know you were a princess I'd think—"

"Don't." She'll sit up and hunch in on herself, and he'll curse his stupid tongue for talking, for being less careful than it should. "Don't. Peter, I can't…"

"I'm sorry," he'll say, and she'll laugh shakily, wiping one hand across her forehead.

"No. Damn it, I always overreact, I should…it shouldn't be so…" her voice fails her. His will too. And then, even while outside they will hear the sirens and automobiles and drones, and the constant beeping of the docking bays opening and closing, he will feel something uncanny, like a brush of that late afternoon in the stone silence.

"We had some good times then," he'll say, at last. "Didn't we?" And it will hurt more that the question needs to be asked at all.

"Of course we did," Bri will answer. Her fingers finding his. Her fingernails pressing a crescent bloom into his untouched skin. The moment where she can't look at him. The moment where he turns away, and picks up his screwdriver again.

She will leave in silence.

Everything wears on you eventually. And though he never tires of *her,* he tires enough of the walls to scratch numbers into them, like a prisoner's dying, prideful plea. He sticks his hands into the roses and they come away bloody and scarred. They do not open for him anymore. There has never been a way out.

He sees her, watching, from the other end of the courtyard, in the shadow of a laughing statue, its curls and the folds of its endless drapery and its frozen flesh. When he walks toward her, she vanishes down one of the halls, and he doesn't see her for hours after that.

"You hate me," she says, when he finds her, sitting on the bed in her room. The embroidery is gold, and tarnished. The curtains are heavy with dust. Shackles of stitched roses seem to engulf her legs. "I told you you would."

"I don't," he says. "It's just that sometimes I need to move, I need to try and I…" He doesn't say *I can't stay here,* because he can, and he will, and he does, and he promised. But it lingers on his tongue like the taste of blood. "But I don't hate you. I never could."

"Even though I brought you here?"

"Even though you called me in my dreams?" he counters, stepping forward, tugging her elbow, pulling her out of her careful, back-turned slouch, and she unfolds warily, like a trap. "When will you really get it in your head that this wasn't your fault? You didn't ask to be put under a spell and you didn't know your dreams would call out to mine. And for the record?" he gives her a challenging grin. "Even if you had, and I had known, I would still have come. So stop…" for a moment, it is hard to breathe, and he finds his smile sliding away. "Stop acting like it means I can't love you more than anything else in the world…"

She presses her hands to her eyes, and her voice shakes. "I just wish," she says, "that I could give you anything more than this."

Someday soon it won't be enough.

Perhaps it already isn't.

But what can they do about it now?

He lies beside her on the thick monstrosity, watching the motes of light fall, and stand, and fall.

It will not always be easy, when they are young. Peter promises to stay, but when they graduate, they have a falling-out, and he leaves for a tour not knowing if he will come back dead. He sends her postcards full of blacked-out words telling her where he is, how much he loves her, how much he is sorry. He never speaks of them.

Bri boasts about her conquests, when he returns for a few meager days; she wears her shirt unbuttoned dangerously low, and watches his eyes stray. "Trying to break more men's hearts than you did in our past life?" he says, only once, in an unguarded moment of cruelty. And the blood leaves her face. And he remembers how many bones he had passed, trying to get in.

You're like a vortex, he wants to scream. *You're a damned curse.*

"I hate you," Bri says, her voice shaking. "You were supposed to be here."

"Maybe I'm a liar," he says, like he's trying it on for size. She stares at him like she wonders if he believes it. He laughs, and it sounds bitter. Rank. He hates that he can't recognize himself and yet everything about her is still so brilliant it cuts him. He hates that he'll fall back toward her the moment he's given a chance. How could he ever choose an entire, empty world without her in it?

"I'm sorry," Bri says, at last, "that I made you a liar."

"It wasn't your fault," he says.

"Yeah," Bri says, sardonically. "I believe you."

And someday he *will* get enough money to buy that airship, and they'll pack their few things and take off, and the plume of scree will shoot out behind them and the gears will crank into oiled life from their hidden, weightless slumber and he will smell something like flames and something like roses.

He won't ask her if she sabotaged the engine, because there's no one else that could have done. He'll watch the skyline below while the dark smoke trails in a wake behind them, and he'll know that up in the clouds, it feels like fog, and rain, and darkness, and there is nowhere beyond the limits of the world, not for them.

At the rail, he'll see her eyes turn to his, and he'll smile. She'll put one hand on the greened bronze and he'll take it, and kiss the back as though he is meeting her for the first time, if their first time in another life had been formal and full of ceremony the way it should have been, and not rushed and full of regrets. If they had been able to stand before the courtiers and dance the night away under a pendulum of stars. In the west, the sun sets with molten sharpness, a thorny cut into the softness of the sky. Every night it slips away again.

The deck will shudder under their feet, and it will become close, the mirage of a furnace making the air waver. "Sorry it couldn't… have been different," Bri will say, and her eyes will be the color of soot, hidden and then revealed by the swirl of her dark hair. "Just once."

Her finger trembles on his lip, and he takes a breath.

Like a halo, an arc of flame behind her.

Noticing

"At this rate, there will be nothing else to watch in twelve years."

For as long as they can recall, the watchers have taken note of what happens to the world, recording everything in weighty scrolls as large in diameter as the equator. They know every weather pattern and every invention of Man. Because there are many things to look upon, they specialize: Shift watches birds. Cormorant, pelican, buzzard and dove. Macaw, toucan, peacock. Around the table with its cloth made of spun clouds, Shift watches the swirls and eddies as the lower end of the pristine fabric trails on the rough floor. It has gone grey at the tips. And every time they meet these days, the grey has traveled higher.

They leave the table when the meeting is over.

"What can we be if we're not watchers?" Brook says. "Am I supposed to only categorize and re-read what has already been?"

No one answers.

Outside the dwindling hall, Shift sees Trace standing with their back to the archway. In the noon sun, they are only a pattern of brightness and shadow, as though something in them, standing against the inevitable, has fissured.

They walk by, Brook and Shift, and as they do Shift catches the emptiness in Trace's gaze and shivers. "Come to the records room with us?" they and Brook ask on a sudden whim.

Trace turns their head, blinking free and seeming somewhat surprised to see Shift standing there. "No, you two go on ahead," they say pleasantly. They walk away.

Next time the watchers meet, Trace is gone. They have pulled themself apart. And they are not the only one to do so. The endless hall is half-empty, and it echoes with the spaces others should be. It is the first time Shift has seen the same destruction that is in the world echoed here, and when they leave the gathering, they falter.

"You won't do that, Brook," Shift says.

"Of course not," Brook says. "I don't think I'll show up again though. It's too awful, seeing…" they fall silent. "Anyway. You know where to find me, in my section of Noticing. There's a good deal to replay." They smile wanly and walk off, waving, swallowed in the endless corridors.

For a moment Shift is alone. Then they pace to the canyon between here and the world, looking down. Below, sky. Below the atmosphere and space, inside the everything that makes up matter. Shift thinks about standing here and watching for twelve more years until there is nothing left but a void, a dark chasm to be stopped up. And they can't.

They take out a needle, and coax the thin cloudlets from the stream between here and the world. Floating pearl, it drifts as they twirl it between their fingers, into something thin and strong. They turn it to thread, and sew a form made of afternoon sunlight. It is a diver, wings bent down, and when they step inside it they fall toward the sea.

~

Shift coughs up water, and blinks. The ground has risen up to meet them, and their perfect form has gotten twisted around. The wings are broken, they think. Something else is wrong with the beak and eyes. They need to walk, but they don't have the right ability to do so; outside the range of their vision Shift can hear a human saying something, over and over again. "It's hurt!" A low, distressed voice. "It's hurt." They look up when the speaker takes them in its hands, carefully, as though cradling their fragile self and smoothing down the spaces where the cloud-thread has broken. A male of the species, with blue eyes. Shift looks into them, wondering how the sky has been captured in a glass, and pieces their form together from pain and the speaker's words. It has a mouth this time and it is human like their rescuer. They become too cumbersome to carry and are set down, but the speaker doesn't stop holding their broken wing, broken shoulder, broken hand.

~

"It was touch and go for a while," says the blue-eyed man.

Shift groans, sitting up and looking over their—his?—new body. It looks akin to their rescuer. Shift feels unsettled. They have never been interested in Man, and less so since they found out that there would be nothing left in twelve years, and Trace died and the infinite hall emptied.

They tell the man this.

"Oh," says the man.

"Oh?" Shift says. "Is that all?" They are feeling angry, a roiling anger like a storm. This species is destroying everything and this man, who rescued Shift, has nothing to say about it but *oh.*

"I thought you were human," the man says.

"You rescued a bird," Shift says. Their voice starts off confident but by the time they finish speaking, their voice has trailed off into uncertainty. "Didn't you?"

The man rubs a hand through his dark hair, and Shift watches the deepness of shadows in it. It is the right color for feathers, this man who is not a bird. "I thought I did," the man admits at last. "But by the time you were here you, well…and I thought maybe I just imagined it. That I was so worried…pieces were warping and I had to think you into being somehow. I think. I've heard of things like that, you know? Magical containers for essence. That's what all bodies are, I suppose. I never thought it was real, but I remembered quilting when I was a kid. My mother would tell me fairy tales when—"

"Why are you telling me this?" Shift asks abruptly, and the man stops speaking.

"I don't know," he says. "Sorry. Uh. You can go in the bathroom if you want. If you think you still need help I can try to call a doctor. I don't know if I can find one, but…"

Shift navigates the room. It is a small, two-bed room with the lights turned down. On one rickety bedside table is a pocket sewing kit with scissors that have fallen apart and thin pink and orange polyester thread on small black plastic spools. The whole thing feels cheap and off-kilter, and when Shift enters the bathroom they turn on the light and flinch at the electric buzz. They close the door behind them, legs shaking, and slide to the floor. They have not seen anything yet. They still feel deflated, and they hate their weak human arms.

Salt-water leaks from their open eyes, as though they are losing the rest of the sea.

"Are you…okay?" a hesitant voice says through the door. It's the blue-eyed man. Shift draws an arm roughly across their face.

"Yes," they say. They stand up, to more fully convince themself, and stagger to the mirror. The human looking back looks much like the blue-eyed man. Hair just the right color for feathers. Shift watches the way the air eddies around it. They have clear blue eyes that are puffed red from crying. They look ordinary dressed in a large t-shirt and a red sweater. What an ordinary man they are.

Underneath their shirt the spot where their wings had broken and the place where their guts had been falling out and the knobbled knees are sewn up with pink and orange thread. Shift brushes a hand across the spot and hisses at the sudden ache of pain. Their fingers come away tipped with blood.

~

"So," says Mikhail.

Shift is walking around the small room, close to the window, looking at the blacktop outside. Through the dull glass and the crosspieces of the shades, it could be nothing but a curio put in a box.

"Twelve years."

"Less, for you," Shift says. "That's just when there will be nothing left to watch at all." They shrug. "For you, it will be more like five."

"And for you I guess," Mikhail says. Shift clenches their fists and watches the skin grow taut under the tension of their anger.

"Yes," Shift says at last. "And for me."

"Is there something you want to do? Before the end?"

Shift shrugs, lowering themself onto the white metal heater. The cold air of the window behind them and the scratching of the thread in the wounds where their wings have been make them grimace. They dig their fingers into the grating, and the soft heat blows upward, drying the tear-tracks on their face. "What about you?" they say.

Mikhail laughs. "Up until yesterday, I was heading for the border."

Shift squints at him.

"To get out of the draft," Mikhail explains, in a quieter voice. He looks away. "I left my country because I didn't want to be killed in the airship battle. It's not that I don't want to…fight. I just don't know what the point is of destroying one of the last habitable cities on earth under the illusion of gaining more ground."

"And you aren't heading for the border anymore?" Shift asks.

"Got across it. Cost me the rest of my money. And now I'm free in no man's land. Outside all the pressure-domes and the hydroponic gardens. I'm hardly going to live for more than six years in the Wastes, considering the pollution. So. One year less isn't bad I guess."

"Isn't bad I guess," Shift echoes. "I was hoping for one lifetime," they admit. They remember their beak piercing the sky as they fell.

"Why not stay where you were?" Mikhail says.

"I don't know," Shift admits, in a whisper just touching the back of their throat. "It seemed…inconceivable."

"We have one more night here," Mikhail says at last. "You should rest."

"I wish I could," Shift says.

The heater is still working, and yet they shiver.

~

The Roman roads are straight and still standing. This is what shows the way into the Wastes beyond every limit. Mikhail has a backpack with his remaining possessions. Shift has the clothes on their back that were once Mikhail's.

The Labrador duck once spent its winters in the shelter of inlets, feeding on mollusks. The males with striking black and white, females with soft brown plumage. It didn't know how to live outside the habitat of its short migrations, and now the only thing that's left is stuffed specimens in museums.

This is what Shift tells him that first day as they walk. They have a pair of ratty sneakers that Mikhail bartered for, because the blue-eyed man had brought with him only one pair of boots. Inside the sneakers, their feet are wrapped in rags. Shift can feel blisters raising, and they look ahead, arms swinging at their sides. The pall of low smoke hasn't left since midday, and the sunset is going to be brilliant.

"One time a man went fishing in the choppy waters," Mikhail says. "This was long ago, you remember. And he saw a woman swimming as though she were flying, like she belonged there. And a sealskin lying on the ground. He took the skin and hid it, and then convinced her to come back with him, where they lived a long and happy life. But one day she found the skin again, in the bottom of a trunk, and took it and left him and their children behind, and jumped back into the waves."

"That never happened," Shift says.

"That's the story the way my mother told it," Mikhail replies, with a shrug. "Maybe the same thing happened to your duck. Maybe it got tired of living stuck in one place while everything fell down around it."

"And maybe it just died."

They walk in silence until the light glances off the standing stones and everything else is bathed in shadow; then they sit. The bloody edge of the grass seems to shimmer. Shift pulls the shoes from their feet, and their needle from their sleeve. They pull the grass free, all cellulose and refracted light and deep reaching roots in what remains of dust. They stitch the sides of their feet, building calluses out of the stubborn things and slip-stitching it into skin. They put the needle away.

Mikhail watches. "I've never seen real magic before," he says, as Shift rubs their toes and arches until the stitches sink under their skin.

"There's no such thing as real magic," Shift says. They push and push, but the ache doesn't leave their sinews and bones. One crooked toe, with a ripped nail, bleeds sluggish and dark.

~

The New Caledonian rail slipped from sight quietly, making its way up the mountains to escape from feral dogs and pigs. Brown with a grey belly and a yellowish bill, it lived in the spaces when sunlight disappeared, twilight or perhaps night.

Shift knows its sound, they had recorded it as they watched, but now that is lost to them, stuck in their section of Noticing. They cannot reproduce it for Mikhail, where they sit curled up around a small fire in a hollow under the stars.

"It's okay," Mikhail says. He takes their shaking hand, brushing his fingers across their palm. "I believe you. Just tell me the rest."

"You don't understand," Shift says. "If I hadn't recorded it there would be nothing left. And there's twelve years left before the end, but I left, when I could have saved others."

"But you wouldn't have saved them," Mikhail says quietly. "Not really. You would have written about them, put them in a library no one visited while your own species committed suicide. And when the universe was empty, what would it matter that you'd found the last bird in the world?"

"You sound very heartless, Mikhail," Shift says.

"I'm realistic," Mikhail says.

"That is how you convince yourself you don't care," Shift says, and turns away.

A hollow, eerie wail throws itself around the stones, the old music of the wind.

"I'm sorry," Mikhail says.

"But you do care," Shift says. They look between the angles of their legs, covered in worn denim. "You saved me. You saw me when I was wounded, and it mattered to you. How can I care any less about what I see?"

"Why not stay, then?" Mikhail says. "Stay and do your duty. Keep everything close."

"Because I couldn't," Shift says, and their heart aches. They press their hands to it, as though fearing for more blood, but there is nothing but long, inward breath. "I couldn't watch it all disappear."

They press their eyelids shut, until all they can do is feel.

~

They cross paths with a band near noon. The Men give them suspicious looks and herd them away from the food wagon. When Mikhail asks about the lay of the land they say, "It's all Wastes from here on out," and laugh.

Mikhail nods and they leave quietly while Shift looks behind at the hard, stained faces and wary eyes.

They walk in silence until the band is out of sight and sound.

"There's safety in numbers," Shift says.

"And competition," Mikhail says. "Surely you know about that."

Shift shrugs. "I don't understand Men," they say.

"Nobody does, I think," Mikhail says. Mikhail has one hand curled around his backpack strap, worrying at the plastic, and he's looking forward when the shots fire. Shift stumbles, and watches the smoke ring its way through the blue-eyed man's shoulder. Mikhail gasps and falls, looking almost surprised, and the Men approach from all sides, eyes on his pack.

Shift grits their teeth and feels something white-hot, stumbling to their feet. At first the Men don't seem to notice; and if they did, what would they care, about an ordinary man swaying on his feet? Shift can't move, can't summon up the strength to walk over, and they see the group bend over Mikhail. They need to act, before the pack is stolen, before Mikhail is killed, but they can't take a step. So they bend their arm; move the T-shirt up and rip the stitches free, sticking their arm inside the hole in their belly, dipping their fingers into the slippery surface of their intestines as blood sluices its way around their elbow, until they have reached just deep enough. And then they *pull,* and the *shadows* come out, something *utterly too big* for the world, something that is meant to remain in the place beyond. They close their eyes and scream. They are crawling out of the skin, and dragging it along behind them like a backpack full of meat. They reach the Men at the same time and slice clean through each throat, six at once, and watch the blood arc its way sizzling onto the ground.

Then Shift is falling, eyes open onto a greyed sky, hand pressed to their stomach, and hurting. Something in their lungs rattles.

"Shift?" Mikhail says. He reaches out. "Shift, look, you can't die on me. Not yet. Five more years, you said, remember?"

Shift chokes. Bubbles crawl up their throat. "I… remember."

They take their needle between slippery fingers and make a shaky running stitch across the wound, using blood and the sharp tang of effluent and *five more years, you promised.*

They think they've figured out how to breathe; they zigzag

fear around the hole in their lungs, pushing the silver needle through until it's closed.

They sit up. Sweat is running over their face, their blood-covered stubble. Their shoulders are tensed and a line of blood is running between their shoulderblades where the gashes from their wings have opened up again.

"We can't stay here," Mikhail says. His face is drawn, and he has a hand pressed to his shoulder. Blood drips between his fingers. Together, they stand.

"The wagon," Shift says.

Mikhail nods, and they make their way back.

There are three men left where the band had been. Three men looking bored and waiting around, not knowing their companions have been killed.

"We'll never get them all," Mikhail says.

"Yes," Shift says, voice hard. "We will." They open their hand for the gun that shot Mikhail.

"Do you know how to use that?" Mikhail whispers.

"No," Shift says. "But it can't be that hard."

Mikhail shakes his head. Propping his injured arm against his chest, he aims, and three men fall in the space between three heartbeats.

"I thought you weren't a soldier," Shift says, quietly.

Mikhail shoves the gun into his open pack. He walks to the wagon, and searches for something to patch himself up.

Later, they sit on the end of the wagon.

Pallas's cormorant used to live across the reaches of the globe, but it's been a long time since then. They are huge, and stand watch on the cliff's edge. Black-winged, green-backed, they avoid flight, and are overrun by men wanting feathers, whales, food, furs. It is not a battle. It is a slow massacre.

Shift tells Mikhail this in rambling loops of speech while Mikhail cries beside them.

"Are you okay," Shift says, interrupting their description of the skeptical look in the seabird's yellow-ringed eyes.

"I'll be fine," Mikhail says. He reaches out his hand and Shift takes it tightly within theirs. Shift raises the hand to their lips and kisses like they could stitch together the hurt. They press their lips to the back of Mikhail's wrist. They kiss like they must never stop touching or they will fall apart.

"I should have known," Shift said. "I should have suspected them when I saw."

"I'm the one who almost got us killed," Mikhail says, "because I wanted to speak to them instead of walking by."

"I guess we both made a mistake," Shift says at last. They pause. "At least we have a wagon now."

Mikhail laughs raggedly, a burst of something that shakes his entire frame, and pulls Shift close.

~

The wagon is a burden. It carries much inside it but it slows their progress to a long rattle that traces ruts of dust in their wake. The only time Shift really likes it is at night, when they stop moving, and curl up inside. The bow-curve of its edges frames the night sky, which is more and more an endless pool of shimmering light, geode-sharp, the further they get into the Wastes. Mikhail tells them about the constellations; Shift looks at the bright points of Seth, murderer of Osiris, being held back by Tawaret; and they feel themself flying with the Geese of Ra as though to follow the spiraling path up, through the edge of the chasm and back to the place beyond the world.

Beyond the ridge of their spine, in the spaces on either side, Mikhail slides his palms along the knotted scars done up in pink and orange thread. "I'm not very good at this," he says quietly, scraping a fingernail against the rolled surface. "When you heal yourself it's like nothing ever happened but this…"

Shift shrugs. "I wouldn't have been able to," they say. "I was dying."

"And now?"

"Like you said, Mikhail," Shift whispers. "You put magic into it. You had to think me into being. I could not get rid of it without taking my body apart, until there was nothing left underneath."

"And if you did," Mikhail says. "Would you be able to go back?"

"I don't think so," Shift says. "Gravity is too strong, you know. And I think… " they fall silent, and feel the impression of heat from Mikhail's chest. With their face turned away they can fall apart soundlessly, and if Mikhail notices he says nothing. Just waits, and breathes. "I've forgotten how I crafted my wings."

~

A flock of passenger pigeons numbered billions, once. Reddish brown, such an unobtrusive color, but the iridescence on the neck and mantle: bronze, violet, green; slate and olive; grey-blue, pink tail, coral feet. Poised and slender, fast and nomadic, with pointed wings; scapula and sternum, and the sound! Raucous cacophonous, *kek-kek, kee-kee-kee-kee, keeho!* How loud the skies were, once! The noon was blotted out to endless darkness, the wings buzzed, and when they moved into a smaller surface, oh how like a dragon, a twisting blizzard, a column of unimaginable depth!

Shift had watched, once, for fourteen hours a flock pass by, and Noted it. It had been, they thought, as infinite and joyous as the watchers. They traveled limitless forests, their weight bending structures and creating it as they lived, until the forests ended, until they were hunted for food and sport. Until the last remnants were gathered where last things always are; prized beyond measure because they are gone.

Some photographs of the captives remain. They watch, still living, though in monochrome; a single speck of what had once been the most numerous bird species in the world.

~

Some nights Mikhail takes the fabric scraps scavenged from the dead they left behind and washed clean in the frozen marshes, and he sews. With a tiny needle like a flash of starlight, in and out of the remains of wool flannel. A red piece is emerging, with a zigzag of blue cuffs tracing below the sky. He outlines the birds

Shift tells him about in orange and pink against a rubicund surface, filling the blank canvas with life.

"The Uprising happened when I was younger," Mikhail says, squinting by the light of the small grass-fed fire. "For three years I lived with my brothers going from house to house, while every day another pressurized dome shattered. I didn't know what it was about then. I didn't know what anyone was fighting for. All I knew was the way the sky looked when it was broken; like this..." he traced a jagged, teethlike structure in front of him. "Dark in front, and even darker behind it, terrifyingly so. Then there were talks of hostages and negotiations and everyone thought maybe this time. You know? But we didn't stop. The cities, I mean, and the machines running them."

"I remember," Shift says. "I counted the seventeen last birds in that year alone."

"And for you?" Mikhail says. "What was it like up there? What is it like? I suppose you never had a childhood, but you have a history, and that means something."

"We had no history," Shift says. "We had yours. Everything you ever did in this world we counted and put meaning to."

"There you go then," Mikhail says. "If you put meaning to it, you made it yours. What stories did you *tell* about us?"

"Why should we need one? The world keeps going, until it doesn't," Shift says. "And when it doesn't, then we lose all our stories. How are we supposed to live with that?"

Mikhail says nothing. He sews, and the sharp point of his needle pierces the fabric, giving it strength, changing it utterly.

Shift continues. "We had a meeting hall made of clouds, endless and infinite. Outside it, we watched. I saw how things were and are; how the first stirrings of uncertainty traveled like the gulf stream. Nothing was untouched. We lost our moorings as what we watched slipped away beneath us. Then the infinite became less. Some pulled themselves apart, becoming nothing. I… bounded myself to this." Shift watches, entranced by flame and Mikhail's eyes, storm-dark. The small, fragile thread pulls upward, the cloth upon his knee framed by his hands.

"Sometimes I wish I'd stayed," Mikhail says, softly. "I cast myself out when I left; I became nothing but a wasteland scavenger untouched by humanity. And all because I didn't care enough. Or perhaps because I was afraid."

"And how was fighting airship battles supposed to save the world," Shift says. They put their chin in their laced fingers, and feel the brush of their ankle against Mikhail's skin.

"I don't know," Mikhail says.

~

Shift takes stone and the sound of the wind wailing and chain stitches it along their arms, when they finally rest, tired from dragging the wagon endlessly behind them. They feel more human than they ever have, something like an ordinary man. Their hands are rough and their lips cracked from the wind and cold, when they and Mikhail find a deep hollow in the mountains. They stop moving while the snow blows in, and Shift feels nothing like a bird at all.

The pot pot chee's wings were brilliant emerald, fading to turquoise; with a yellow and orange head. It thrived in swamps and rivers in ancient forests, and of all parrots had the northernmost range. They ate toxic seeds and so they too, were toxic. The forests were eaten away, and those that returned to their dead and dying kin were killed. But the final disappearance of the species, over hardly a decade, and what wiped them out, could not be traced.

In the same cage as Martha, the last remaining passenger pigeon; went Incas, a captive died after his mate. So many lasts.

Shift thinks about captivity. About being a migratory creature confined to one place. The sun seems to slip out of reach with winter, and it is hard for Shift and Mikhail to find enough food to survive. They think about themself, and about Mikhail, and Mikhail's favorite brother, who he tells them about one afternoon when the snow sheets down like a soft blanket, twisting its way into the hollow opening of their cave.

"The child is odd, you know? And what can you do about it," Mikhail says. "My mother explained it to me that way. About changelings, creatures that were just different and living here. Some try to kill it in hopes they'll get back what they had. Others will trick it away, and they'll have nothing. Some few notice and raise the child as their own, and gain good luck. But one day, someone will come by and the child will say, 'Look, there's my parents;' jump over the fence and walk away. That's what my eldest brother did. He did it to gain a title and a position that saved the lives of my other brothers, gleaming medals and honors that two years later meant nothing. He was a hero for two days and a traitor the rest."

"Are you angry at him?" Shift says.

"How can I be?" Mikhail says. "He saved us. How can I be. Even if I want to?"

Shift thinks about kinship as they sew the memory of Mikhail's brother, his hard practicality and his oddness, into their chest with a blanket stitch up the curve of their ribs. Their needle slips through flesh leaving pinpricks of blood behind, and Shift thinks about how lately, every push of the needle hurts more. They think about their skin growing around them, working on its own like the machine it is, despite their own efforts, and wonders where the spark of their own self has hidden.

Everything they sense seems dulled.

"Four more years," Shift says, as they pull their red sweater close. Mikhail takes their hands and rubs them until their fingers warm and uncurl.

"Do you think we'll live to see the end of the world?" he says.

"What's the end of the world?" Shift whispers.

~

The difference between watching twelve more years of everything vanish and living four more years moment by moment is the difference between flying above the sea and drowning in it.

The Mohoidae family is dead. Feeding on nectar, the small songbirds are black and yellow, brown and spotted white.

The Oloma'o hasn't been seen in years, since the mosquitos on the islands.

The black-lored waxbill lived within two thousand kilometers, and didn't go extinct as much as was not sighted again.

The po'o-uli, with its black head and body of silvery-grey, was smaller than a hand. Because of mosquito-borne disease, they were forced upward, because they lost food, because of pigs and mongooses, cats and rats.

Shift is not fond of cats, rats, and dogs; just the way they are not fond of humans. But they do not have to be a cat, a dog, or even a mosquito. Instead, they are a human, with black hair the perfect color for feathers and snow-shadow eyes. They like the look on them much less than on Mikhail, who, when he sings in front of the fire late in the evening, seems as unconquerable as a bird's glance, with strong arms and a back meant for holding. If they could give Mikhail wings, Shift thinks, then both of them could ascend into the white sky and leave the world behind. Shift could show Mikhail the halls of the infinite, and introduce him to their section of Noticing with its perfect records, so unlike the messy stories and tales told from Mikhail's sweet mouth.

But Mikhail has no wings, and the spark within him can't be dragged free of his body. Mikhail is a Man, and his species will be extinct in four years. Perhaps this cave is Shift's own zoological space, where they can watch him exist while everything of his kind in the wild shrivels and dies. Perhaps they will be the last together, undocumented and alone, and will slip into extinction quietly, without being Noticed at all.

And perhaps, Shift thinks, that is important too. There will not be tales told, there will not be taxonomies, but there will always be this: some kind of mystery in the heart.

❋

Entanglement

You didn't know, that first long, rainy evening, under the flash of wet pavement—the glare of red, yellow, and a fading, bruised orange—what would become of it all. Only saw him and in that dark suit he looked untouchable, ice-chip eyes and breath that fogged out, like yours, did. You should have known then, though the space between your orbit was eternal, an uncrossable distance, that all it would take was a step.

But you talked of war.

While others you knew had waited in open fields and under the chequered lighting of cafés, and could draw each other in charcoal, you felt the shadow of zeppelins overhead. Each night was filled with the rumble of troops marching by, and when the volcano joined them, and ash rained down into a black snow, in the cold air, you stood and raked your boots through the corrupted slush and breathed in dust.

He knew more of guns. In fact, when you saw the way his fingers touched the gleaming oil, each perfect, mechanical, tainted part, he added an unstoppable perfection to the machine, waiting between each *click* of the barrel, between each concrete wall. In the silence after, when the blood had already stopped, when you took inventory, you realized how that space had contracted to the barest inch, and did not even wonder at it. But it was years, still, until the touch of your fingers; though your dreams had already bled into watercolored ground.

"This was a mistake," you said, when from the top of the spire you stood with nothing but cold air below you and an endless city, grimed and unreal, fevered. The wind was harsh and it would have taken nothing to fall backward into air.

"Perhaps," he said, and you realized with something like grief that even he had been worn down, still as marble, smudged with ink. *I thought you were perfect,* you didn't say, because you knew perfection was something that had never been in the cards for you. *Leave me,* you could have said, and almost did, but your selfishness stayed you. *It was a mistake,* you said, and let him draw his own conclusions.

Perhaps, he said. *But there's no mistake I'd rather have made.*

The deafening silence, and years later, you wake to the world after a war. You wake to the sound of footsteps into new mud, and a clean rain, and he is closer, like a refracted mirror, and as fleeting as the flash of light from the corner of a CD, casting shadows on the ceiling. You figure out how to touch, the way ordinary people do, with the performance of casualness; but you can feel the crumbling abyss underneath, and the weight of your casualties stretching out behind you like rows of headless men. It's nothing that will ever fit you, but perhaps that's not so bad. Perhaps being a mis-turned wheel in a spinning globe is only as it should be after all, when in the spring, the scent of mint and apple blossoms fills the acres behind you.

Sometimes, when the top has stopped spinning, you throw the dice again. Sometimes it ends. And it ends. And:

So many years ago, you remember seeing him, from a far distance, and you were struck with the foreknowledge that to you he would forever be everything, and nothing at all.

I love you, he said, once. And the world, which sometimes went on, fractured into streams within the space of a moment, the whirl against a boulder, an unfathomable array: a quiet.

After it all, you try to remember how it happened, how that beam of light which was the two of you, existing in the state of all and not, wave and particle, finally fell to pieces, and whether the fact that others were watching changed a single thing.

You said nothing.

You said: *I love you too.*

In the night, when you reach across the bed to find only void, what terrifies you is the finality of your own answer.

You don't remember if you opened your mouth at all.

✺

The Day Before Tomorrow

i.

It was autumn, during the days when the air was sharp enough to chew. Walking down the cracked asphalt road, Min kicked a cragged stone back and forth from one shoe to another. In between, there was the unmistakable sound of footfalls, muffled with the rubber tread, and there, the skittering of the stone, and the occasional wet smear of it sinking across a span of leaves, brown and veined and already worn down to shadows.

"How did you do on the test?" she said at last, in a tone of conversational nonchalance. She peeked at her companion, who was walking heedless of the chill in the same combination of T-shirt and jeans she always did.

"Dunno," Pari replied.

"I wasn't sure about the last question," Min confessed. They stopped at the crossroads, and from that corner they could see down the curve of the street, the edge of the road marked with its zipping stark power lines, the immense curled swathe of trees broken intermittently by the pale painted sides of houses and spires. It was noon, and the sun was hot, so that in moving from the shadows under the trees to the open space Min felt a shiver even under her sweater and scarf.

"I think it was C," Pari said. The girls stood for a moment, unwilling to go their separate ways. A car sped by round the curve with a rumble of noise and presence, and then everything subsided again. A leaf fell, and Min and Pari both reached forward to catch it, and missed. It twisted to the ground, and lay, a spark of orange at their feet.

"Come get ice cream with me?" Min said.

"At this time of year?"

"Why not?"

Pari shrugged. "Okay."

They took the other turn, continued along the curve of the road that wound its way into town. Pari stuck her hands in her pockets. "Why do you think no one talks about it?" she asked, as though the question had been on her mind for a long time. "—Because they're afraid?"

"Maybe?" Min said. She frowned, and as though both struck by the sudden, unfightable urge, they looked up—over the brick top of the water tower, where: it was. There it was. A mass of dark buzzing, an ink-drenched shadow, a pure midnight. It was, they knew, filled with the sounds of waves, but only the thinnest tendrils held it to the ground. It filled the whole eastern expanse. It covered the farthest reaches of the mountain. It held drops of water suspended in its reach, and the ground underneath it was ash and dead bones.

Pari swallowed. She looked away first. And Min, gazing, felt its sound, that sound that everyone knew, for it crept into their dreams: that endless beating pulse. It was closer than it had been even yesterday; or larger: she still recalled how the roads in that direction trailed off into melted rubble, a volcanic interruption.

"Maybe it's angry?" she said.

"Does it get angry?" Pari said.

Min chewed on a strand of hair, an anxious habit. She looked away and smiled back at Pari. "Who knows," she said. They laughed, and turned the next corner.

They were almost in the valley, now, and *it* was barely more than a spot of endless night, an unfathomable pinprick, like someone had punctured the sky. Blue shone, and the dappled light of the sun played over their sneakers.

By the ice cream shop, they read the chalked sign. Pari decided to get pineapple. Min got chocolate. They paid, and were then returned to the doorstep, ice cream in hand; Pari stuck her spoon into her cup and balanced on the curb. Min sat down beside her. In the emptiness under their feet, the hollows of the road's intestines were filled with water.

Past went Mrs. Johnson, their teacher. They said hi.

"Did you hear that Patti broke up with her boyfriend yesterday?" Min said.

"Huh, really?" Pari asked. She flopped down beside her friend.

"Mm-hm," Min said. "He was a jerk to her anyway, so it's a good thing."

"Daniel's getting married," Pari said.

"Wow."

They finished their ice cream and threw away the cups and spoons.

"See you tomorrow?" Min said.

"If we're still here," Pari joked. Min knocked her with her elbow, laughing.

"Sure, I'll meet you by the steps."

ii.

In winter, everything was ice. It hung from the eaves in long, thick, glistening spikes, like a burning-glass for the weak sun. Min wrapped her scarf around her, put on her coat and mittens, and walked across the grey road. Aames, the neighbour, was using a snowblower. It cut through the silence; he looked down, concentrating, at the dusty whirl by his feet. The sound chased her down the street.

At the corner, by the steps, Pari was waiting. She had her hands tucked into the pockets of her jeans, boots on that she stomped, with concentrated precision, into the roadside slush. Goosebumps trailed their way across her bare arms, and when she turned to Min, the breath of her air made a clear puff that hung, suspended, and drifted away. "Hi, Min."

"You should wear your coat," Min said.

Pari shrugged. "Don't want to."

"Take my scarf at least?"

Pari shrugged, and took it, looping it around her neck. "I'm not cold," she said.

"Still."

"Do you think they'll solve anything?"

"At this meeting?" Min frowned. "Well, they've got to start somewhere. That's why it's a town hall? Right?" Pari held out a hand and Min took it as they poked their way over sidewalks slippery with black ice.

They could hear the steady sound of water rushing by underfoot, under the cusp of the road. The manhole covers and the drains, full. When they walked by too slow, sometimes they could see just-a-bag-of-bones crawl out of it; a very long, tail-like creature with legs and no eyes or mouth, but a nose. It turned their way, sniffing, and they hurried into the lighted areas as dusk fell deeper over the town. It followed, its skeletal fingers dragging on the ground, like a scraping knife, but stopped at the corner of Main Street and wouldn't come any further.

The town hall was lit up with warmth, gold light spilling out through the doors, the glass windows diamond-paned, reinforced by wires. Inside, they hurried to find seats in the girth of folding chairs spread out into an army of aluminum points. Pari sat down, jiggling her leg. Her hands twisted around the ends of Min's scarf.

Jacob and Emily slid in beside them, at some point, Jacob pulling out a seat for Emily. She smiled at Jacob and kissed him, gently, on the mouth. "I hope they talk about the water," Emily said, leaning away to flop onto a chair. "It's been rusted for weeks. Hi, girls." She put her purse in between her feet and fished around for a tissue to wipe the fog from her glasses.

"Hi," Min said. Pari was leaning back, thinking about the long entry she'd added to her journal yesterday, her eyes closed to muffle the sound of people arriving, chattering, filling up the empty room with keys clinking and the scrape of chair legs across the floor. Min nudged her. "Emily and Jacob say hi."

"Hi," Pari said, eyes still closed.

Jacob flipped through a brochure for the new Rapid Water Adventure down the road. His chipped blue nail polish covered the image of a screaming group of friends in a log.

"Pari and I want to talk about the bone things," Min said.

"Those?" Jacob said distractedly. "They're harmless."

"I know, but they draw in the alligators," Min said. "And I really don't want to get eaten by one of *those*."

"True," Jacob said. "You should mention that when you bring it up." He stared down at the open brochure in his hand. *Laugh like your life depends on it!* it said. The people in the brochure had colorful shirts on and tans. They glowed with tourist-bound enthusiasm.

"It's not even open yet," Min said, following his gaze.

"Just wondering if there'll be one of those big slides," Jacob said. "The kids have been asking about it all week."

Near the front of the room, the meeting was beginning. Jacob slid the brochure into the side pocket of Emily's purse. The corner stuck up, making an odd, upside-down picture of someone's sandaled foot, water tugging at the ankle.

iii.

In the spring, Rosa and Juan from down the block moved west—they'd heard it was nicer in the country.

It was a lowering cloud over the east, so that whenever Min woke up early in the morning from the birds' racket, she could see it from her window behind the roofs of the houses. It was up against the water tower now, and its dark underbelly cast a shadow over the bulbous white roof. Sometimes she almost thought she could feel it, a vibration rattling her bones. Min could never tell if she wanted to leave her shades closed, and not have to look, or open them to let in the sun. Sometimes she left her shades open only a crack, and then the sunlight would steal in like a burning lance across the floor.

Min put on the new shirt she'd bought last weekend, with the magnolias on it. She put a yellow hair band onto her wrist, and then added a few more for good measure, in shades from blush to neon pink. She raced through two granola bars and called that breakfast, running to meet Pari in the park.

When she got there, Pari was staring at a roly-poly bug.

"Hi, Pari," Min said.

"Hey," Pari said. She was squatting on the ground, the ends

of her jeans dragging in the mud. She poked her finger at the bug and it curled up. "Did you know they're related to shrimp?" Pari said. "They have gills and everything."

"But they're on land," Min said.

"Yup." Pari looked up at her and grinned.

"How long have you been poking that thing?" Min asked.

"I dunno, since I got here," Pari said. The bug had uncurled, a little grey knight in armor. Pari poked it again, gently, and it curled up, frozen in its fear. Pari stood up and dusted her hands on her jeans.

"I've never seen you wear that shirt before," Pari said.

"It's new," Min said.

"Oh." Pari nodded. She rocked forward on her toes. One shoelace, untied, fell around her blue and white sneakers. "Uh, it's nice."

"Thanks," Min said. "I thought, since we were going to the movies later—" she stopped short, awkwardly. "Well. I mean. That makes it sound like a date."

Pari shrugged. "If you like it, wear it."

"That must be what you do all the time," Min teased, smiling.

"I think I've got some nice clothes around," Pari said. She paused. "Somewhere."

They started walking. In the park, the green things were creeping up out of the dirt. The air had its own smell, Pari noticed. She tried to categorize it, to figure out how it was different from winter. Something fuller, perhaps. More *in* it. She came to this conclusion every year, but it still surprised her.

"Hey, Pari," Min said at last, when they had been walking around an opening hydrangea. She spoke down, looking intently at the flowers. "Have you ever thought about it? Dating? Us, I mean."

"Not really," Pari said. "Why, do you want to?"

Min hesitated. She chewed her lip. "I don't think so. I just had a feeling—well, maybe we should? Right?"

"Because…" Pari said.

"Because otherwise, we're just—" Min fell silent, awkwardly. She stared at Pari as though she'd said something she didn't want to, or maybe *hadn't* said something she *did* want to. Pari's eyes slid away as she thought. She looked at the frilled top of Min's shirt, noticing the braid on it, a loop of machine stitching.

"Nothing wrong with 'just'," Pari said. "Is this about Patti?"

"Maybe," Min sighed. She seemed more at ease now, and Pari decided she'd gotten it right. "She's just been going on and on about how nice it is, now that she found Amy and they're thinking about buying an apartment and, well, that's all of us, isn't it?" She counted on her fingers. "Daniel, Patti, Ethan, you and—and me. They're off doing, well…" she shrugged. "What everyone does."

"I don't care about what everyone does," Pari said. "If you wanna date so you can brag about it, we can. Or you don't even have to date me. You could just tell everyone we're doing it. It's not like they'd be surprised."

"Could I?" Min said, anxiously. "Just tell them, I mean. Without us having to be different, you know."

"Yeah, why not?" Pari said.

"Good," Min said. She smiled.

They walked a little further. At some point, the footpath crossed a small stream, only a few feet deep, planned and directed with nicely-placed stones at auspicious intervals. The water was still rusty. It flowed through, reddish and slow, and Pari dropped a few sticks into it and watched them sink.

Min sat by the edge of the bridge beside her friend, leaning her arms on the lowest bar and swinging her knees off the edge so her feet arced out over the water. The shadows of her legs were dark on the rippled surface.

iv.

It was summer, hot and dry. Even the air was sticky, and the grit in Min's eyes never seemed to leave. She stood at the edge of the hill, realizing this would be her last view from the school, and she looked over the deep green sea of leaves, and the spires of the houses below. Beside her, Pari tapped the end of a smiley-face pencil against her jeans.

"Feeling victorious?" Pari said.

"I don't think so," Min said. "I don't know what I'm feeling. I mean … you know?"

"Yeah," Pari said. Without talking, they looked over at *it*. It had moved, somehow. Imperceptibly, and scorched the ground around the water tower. It was close enough, now, that Min could hear waves all the time. They had tormented her throughout her timed essay, and she hoped she'd managed to write something that didn't sound like a dead sea.

"What now?" Min said.

"I've got a car," Pari said. "We could just…drive away."

"Where would we go where it can't follow?"

Pari pulled her eyes away, turning her back brazenly to the shadow. She stuck her pencil behind her ear. "Doesn't have to be about it. Could be about us."

"Hm," Min said. She turned around, mirroring her friend's posture, and watched their twinned shadows merge. "You mean, sticking together?"

"Of course," Pari said. "I mean—" for the first time she seemed a little hesitant. "There's no one else you want to stick with. Right?"

"Yeah," said Min, softly. "Let's go then."

They walked down the hill. Stepping over the cracked asphalt, Min kicked a stone back and forth between her feet, and then aimed, sending it across the paved expanse and into the sere, soft grass.

✺

It's Already Too Late

House on a hill. River down below. And the rains speckling the grass, dots of cold, salt-ocean. We lived in this house, and from the window we saw: myriad flowers, vermillion, rubicund. The weeping willow dipped its branches low. The paved roads stretched on to the horizon. And down in the low valley, sparkled. And the reeds.

Now the water kept rising, just a bit, and the air was thicker and hotter than it had been. Down in the village we heard crying, we heard dying, but still on the lawn near the road under the haze of sprinklers we could look forward to an endless filmstrip lighting up. "Do something, do something,"

Oh you poor things, it's already too late.

We put on our striped bathing suits and went down to the pool. Hot sun scorching, casting down a black line of our shadows, insects buzzing. Might as well make the best of it while we have it. Eyes closed we splashed water in our faces; it dried our skin with the acrid smell of chlorine, sun-drenched summer. Toes in the dirt. Never end, never end.

Down the road we heard the tornados shriek and the wind rattled the house's bones. Like the kiss from a stranger, shivering, cooling the sweat on our backs. "Do something, do something," the fish in the sea were turning over. It wasn't our fault, why should we fix it? You fix it. Anyway, it's already too late.

Saw the flowers wilt, plugged in the hoses from the dry ground. Saw something poking out of the ground. Bones in oil in the sand pit. We stood there with our toes in it. Stood there and couldn't say a thing. *We never liked playing here anyway.*

"Do something, do something."

"What are we supposed to do? It's already too late."

Did you know the name of the frog that lay upon your front porch yesterday? The one that you tripped over, crackling? No, it wasn't there. No, it was just a frog. They only vanished, and I never heard them anymore, we said, we don't know why; (we sprayed the lawns to keep them clean, and ignored the piles of textbooks. "Do something, do something," but all they ever told us to do was go to the rainforest and shout, they never told us the names of the frogs by the pond, and why the village was so far behind a haze of smoke.) We could hardly see out, but still, from the top floor the whole expanse was almost like an inverted bowl, a drop of water shimmering on a leaf, an ant's world.

Then the village went up in smoke, and we saw the line of cars snaking its way through the ash. "Do something, do something," we heard shouts, shouts—who are they shouting at? We didn't do anything wrong. Talk to the people who made the plastic deck chairs. We bought water bottles and left them on the porch, and behind the porch we burned bonfires and laughed. "It's already too late!"

Then the cracked earth went up to our doorstep. The river was too high, but our toes were caked in mud. The windows had blown out, so we took to a boat. Oars out, we reached for Mars. In the nighttime, the sky was silent. The boat cracked, the water poured in spurts, covering our feet. We could have taken off our coats and plugged the gaps, but then again— it's already too late.

So we lie down, what else is there to do, we take out our bottles, and, dripping, let the water sludge its way over elbows, hips, eyelashes: we look upward; the black is endless, the eye of the storm stretches on a forever moment. Drops splash down on our arms like summer cooling thirst—

✵

The Shivering Ground

They walked the halls of the underground building, listening to footfalls echo from clean floors, each step like a shot. Interspersed, painted slightly cracked plain white, were doors that locked from the outside. The ceiling lights buzzed. And the guard hooked their fingers into the belt of their uniform, staring straight ahead and humming tunelessly as they pushed along the cart. *Lully, lulley, lully, lulley!* At some doors they stopped, took out a tray, and walked inside to give the prisoners food, and out again, locking the door. The keys jangled, and the rattling cart's wheels screeched with a metallic *thunk-thunk-eeeee!hiss.* They reached the end of the hall and paused. The special case was here. Solenoid down, and for the first time *our* side had managed to capture one, and it was still alive. Wouldn't give a name, of course, or any information about the enemy, but there was hope, still, wasn't there. Well. The guard didn't worry about that. They just made sure the doors were locked and everyone who was still there, not dead, got food. They hadn't checked the solenoid yet though, the enemy had been dragged in around three this morning and he'd only just been processed.

The guard stopped the cart. Last tray there, last thing they had to do before going home. Not bad. They turned the key in the lock, pushed open the metal door and stepped inside. There he was. Lying on the pallet under the deep recessed window, face tilted to catch the spot of sun that would be gone by midday. Without armor, only in prison slacks and torso mottled purple, rusty green and lined with deep scratches, blood in his tangled hair. Still he was intimidating and no wonder: wrapped around the cell, folded awkwardly and yet still scraping the ceiling and walls were the wings. Chained to the wall, so he couldn't use it to beat forward, crash people off guard. But he glanced at the door, haughty, a carelessness in his brown eyes.

The guard set the tray down within reach and stepped back.

"So you're the entertainment around here," said the solenoid.

The guard turned to go without speaking. That was their job, anyhow; just check up on the prisoners, see that they were fine, and leave. But they remembered how the prisoner had refused to talk *since*—well, no one wanted to think about that trouble. The guard had never actually been ordered not to speak with the prisoners, but what it would do to your head when you did, they thought. Still. The prisoner had spoken for the first time *since*.

"Yeah, that's me," the guard said, turning back around. Watched, standing, from a safe distance.

"I don't think much of you."

"Eat your swill, solenoid." The creature grimaced, reaching to the tray and poking at the bowl of what was it unenthusiastically. He took one index finger, dipped it into the mush, pressed it to his tongue and spat toward the guard's feet.

"Mhm, you're going nowhere with an attitude like that."

"I'm going nowhere anyway." The solenoid stared down into his bowl. He turned it a few times round on the tray, a gentle momentum scraping its way across the polished surface. Tin reflections scattered on the bare wall.

"What, you don't think you'll be rescued?"

"Is that what you're all hoping for?" the solenoid said. "You'll have to wait a while. I'm no one of importance, a replaceable bit."

"Sure."

The solenoid pressed his bare feet together, toe to ankle, the chains pulled, *rat-tat-shick-shik-shish* and he stopped, pressed his fingers to the bottoms of his feet as though to massage away the pain. "You know I'll tell you nothing."

"I'm not your interrogator. Just a guard."

"You have a name, guard?"

"You have a name, solenoid?"

The solenoid looked ahead; both sets of eyes met across the space. One by the door, the other by the wall, and in between, the empty concrete ground, cool and smooth. Those wings were a deep and brilliant kingfisher blue, filling the bare walls like stars scattered underwater—the solenoid's smile was rueful, and he shrugged.

"Guess not," the guard said. They stepped back, nodded. "See you tomorrow, solenoid."

"See you tomorrow, guard."

The guard walked home. It was a mistake, the guard thought, to have talked to a prisoner. In ordinary times, perhaps that would've been easier to remember. There were precious few prisoners left now. Just three. One never did do anything but sit and stare, the other was feral. It had been a long time since our side had a win, and the city reflected it; from outside the complex there were just miles of barbed wire and inside cracked pavement and a few run-down stores and low twisted oaks parched by drought. The only things left with color in them were the constant billboards, paper ones put up last month when the new mayor wanted to promise better times ahead. The side to the north was bombed out rubble and chemical fires. The guard walked around the dead ends easily, steering through the center of the streets, weaving around packed slow-moving vehicles and listening to the radios blaring the newest pop hits. Catchy tunes, sometimes. Off-duty, they wore no uniform. Went to the deli by the block and ordered Elly's homemade sandwich. "Thank you, ma'am." Then went to the spot by the grimed-up window. Only three seats in the whole place really, it was not much bigger than the solenoid's cell: another reason they shouldn't have talked to him. They were taking it home with them already. No call to be thinking about things like the prisoner right now.

Past the window ran a group of children playing hoops and sticks, whooping and laughing. The guard stared out; startled when Elly walked over to hand a cracked, sturdy mug their way. Coffee on the house. "Funny to think of," she said. "I remember when my…" she stopped, shrugged, and they took the coffee from her, a sip of bitterness. Put it down. *Clink. Tap.*

"Not much else to do, is there," the guard said.

"Surely you've got plenty to do, up in the complex," Elly said. "It must be busy. So many important things going on."

"Mhm."

So many important things going on. The guard wondered about that. Climbing up the steep steps that crawled up the side of another building to the roof and ducking under the hatch. Inside, the room was just as it always was. Rugs on the floor to keep away the chilled nights, rags in the cracks in the windows. A big stereo system with frayed cords across the floor and a few open boxes of books, categorized by age. They sat down on the creaking bed, picked up the lute and plucked a few strings, echoing somewhat in the silence, harsh and clear. *Lully, lulley, lully, lulley!* They toed off their shoes, stood up, started to pace out a choreography for a dance no one would ever play. It was nothing more than a hobby, now, though once it had been the guard's life: this music. No space or place for that anymore for years, now, but they stood on the roof under the sun and played the beginning of a new song while the early stragglers made it past; then lay down on a few blankets and dozed until it got late.

~

Night now and the city was a different beast: half-fearful parties going on behind courtyards put glimmering lights into the deepness of the sky. The guard took a car, waiting two hours for the slow crawl toward the complex. They could've lived there but that would've been too much, so here it was back and forth every night and morning. There were just sounds and floodlights, and the guard showed their pass and stepped into the halls again. They'd had a dream they couldn't quite remember but it reminded them of the song, some kind of significant images going hazy around the edges, but they knew the best way to catch it was not to focus too much. They swept the halls, cleaned the cells and took the prisoners into the washroom one by one. It was complicated with the solenoid; not complicated like with the feral one, who'd just as soon maul you with rotting teeth, but the logistics of the bound wings dragging their ball and chain that had to be unhooked from the wall before the solenoid could stand. Though not so much even then.

"Something wrong?"

"My legs won't carry me. I'm sure someone's put it in the report." The guard knew there must be a report somewhere, the soldiers who'd brought the solenoid in seemed like the type to make reports and they knew protocol asked for that. But no one showed a thing to the guard. It was possible the solenoid was faking, and wanted to make a run for it. But when the guard pressed a hand to the solenoid's thigh there were some kind of bandages there, a deep wound that became clear when the solenoid pulled down the wrappings enough to show the clotted blood.

"I'm putting this all back for a bit while I get something that can carry you," the guard said with a sigh, looking at the contraptions around the wings: four separate sets of chains to hook at various points into the wall. They had a bludgeon in their belt just in case and saw the solenoid eyeing it; but they'd been watchful, and perhaps the solenoid knew it was useless, even if he had some half-formed fancy to take the thing and strike the guard down with it. His wings had been pinioned, so that left the solenoid with no way to escape. The guard walked down the hall, long echoing *thud, thud,* the *rattle-shick* of keys in the supply closet. The only thing with wheels was the food cart, but it would have to do while the guard put in a requisition. And who knew how long *that* would take to be filled. They'd have better luck buying something on their own money. They pushed the cart along, the rattle making the feral prisoner jump up and shriek—growling, half-formed threats, wild-eyed. This was a dead-end prison in a dead-end city, and there was no release in the cards for any of the creatures. Terrible to feel sorry for them, when one had assassinated kings and the other worked with explosives; defectors the lot of them, but the guard had never been able to ask them why they'd done it. The feral one was already mad and the other had been silent since arrival, almost ten years ago.

They unhooked the chains again, four for the dazzling blue wings, two for each leg, and hooked them around the cart instead, watching the solenoid push himself onto the top with a grunt. The cart rattled and shook and screeched but held, sturdy enough. Then they went back down the hall. *Thunk-thunk-eeeee!hiss thwump-boom. Thwump-boom.* The feral one started howling.

"Bit of a dump here," the solenoid said. "And quite empty, it seems."

"Ask the other guard your pointed questions."

"The other guard does nothing but give me a tray of food. Didn't come up with this. Just left me in the cell when I couldn't follow."

The guard shook their head, disgusted.

The solenoid was still eyeing the bludgeon in their belt. And the feral one screeched: *oryaeghahajghhhhao…*

"You want to get to know it a little more? I can oblige but if we keep things civil there's no need."

"Just amusing myself with scenarios," the solenoid said, shrugging. "You know how the boredom gets."

"Talk to yourself, then."

"Not when there might be ears listening."

"Sing to yourself."

"And add to the wonderful racket?" the solenoid smirked, opened his mouth and made an echoing call that shot forward high above the feral howl through the hall. Piercing and ruined, a long ululation that sent shiversome *aiaiaio* down through the empty white panes of the walls like tapestries, battle-cry emptiness. And looked toward the guard as though hoping the guard would scare bone-deep-rattle-horror.

The guard just looked back, nonplussed.

Lully, lulley, lully, lulley! they added, to the racket waking up the shivering ground: *oryaeghahajghhhhao…thunk-thunk-eeeee!hiss thwump-boom. Thwump-boom. Aiaiaio! Lully, lulley, lully, lulley!*

The solenoid held out his arms and swayed. Sat throat open, brown eyes shut, shoulders relaxed and strong, calling, calling, calling— then opened his eyes. Smiled at last, bitterly, and as though startled, even the feral howl went quiet. "You know music, then."

The guard stopped the cart in the washroom, unhooked the chains and let the solenoid pull himself to the bench before turning on the water and turning around. "We'll have to redo those bandages, too," they said.

"No doctor?" the solenoid interpreted the guard's silence behind the *shh, shh, shh* of pounding water. "Ah, not anymore. So this outpost really is abandoned."

"How many humans have you killed, solenoid?" the guard asked, watching the bare walls and the gaping, zigzag crack crawling from the floor.

"Too many to count. I was terribly good at it. I would kill you, you know, if it would do any good. But I wouldn't murder you."

"Mhm," the guard said. They looped one hand through their belt. The other rested on their bludgeon, and they waited through the rest of the shower, both in silence.

~

They hooked the wing chains back onto the cart: *clink-thud. Clink-thud. Clink-thud. Clink-thud.* Unhooked the leg irons. Then while the bandages were still off and dripping with bloodied water over the solenoid's leg, they doused a swab with antiseptic and pressed it against the wound. "It's broken open again," the guard said.

"When I move," the solenoid replied. He pressed his teeth

together against the pain for a moment before continuing. "It happens."

Wet now, and not caked with blood, the solenoid's red hair was darker, curling down over his ears, across his brow. His hands clenched and unclenched, reaching in small increments toward the bludgeon at the guard's belt, before the guard pressed one hand down against his creeping wrist. "Stay still," they said matter-of-factly. They wrapped a new roll of bandages around the solenoid's leg, and helped him struggle into a clean pair of pants. The bruising around his ankles, where the irons had been, was even deeper. Raw metal. The guard wrapped more bandages around his ankles before clamping the irons back on.

"That wasn't necessary, guard," the solenoid said, watching intently when the guard stood back up.

"It wasn't unnecessary," the guard said.

"Hm." The solenoid was quiet on the way back to his cell, though the clatter of the cart made enough racket. The feral one didn't join in this time. When the guard had finished hooking up each wing chain the solenoid said, as though he'd been thinking for a while, "If you'd been captured by my side, guard, we'd have killed you quickly."

"Yes, I know," the guard said.

"A kindness given to our enemies." The solenoid leaned forward, chest cleaned of some of the blood, some of the smaller scratches but still an ocean of unnatural colors radiating from the splotched middles of bruises; long, thin cuts and deep scratches, some newer than they'd been yesterday, to match the curve of the solenoid's fingernails. A bruise across his jaw that had been a sickly purple yesterday now carried bile tones. "Tell me, guard—do you think you're doing me kindness?"

"No," the guard replied.

The solenoid leaned back then, and nodded. He pressed his feet together, wrapping his hands close to the ankle and tracing the bandages under the iron chains. "Thank you."

The guard left, locked the door: *click!* And pushed the cart back down the hall. Thudding feet. The screech of wheels against the floor.

~

They did not manage to think about the song for the rest of that day. All the discordant noises bumped up against each other. When they pushed the tray of food in to the one who wouldn't speak. When they pushed the tray of food in to the feral one and warned the prisoner back with the bludgeon. When they pushed the tray of food in to the solenoid.

"Hello, guard," the solenoid said. He was lying on his stomach, his wings rustling above him, moving incrementally as the guard entered, an open and closed flutter.

"Hello, solenoid."

"Swill again."

"The other guard told me you didn't eat it."

"I didn't."

"Will you?"

"No."

"Do you plan to die?"

"Of course."

The guard watched the solenoid, and the solenoid watched the guard. His head tilted, a slight smile on his face. They didn't know when the interrogators would be back. If ever. The solenoid knew that too, after today. The complex was on the edge of everything, and the years of battle were behind, now, leaving only skirmishes in the ruins. How strange it must be, the guard thought, to have fought and fought your whole life only to realize the battle will soon be over and you will neither win nor lose. At least as a mere guard, and a musician before that, they'd only had to observe, sensing the change in the wind. The solenoid reached for the bowl of swill and tilted it, gently, from his fingertips, the edge of the bowl against the tray. The slop congealed, encroaching over the side of the bowl, gelatinously pooling on the tray's surface, and then the solenoid flipped the bowl over so it lay upside-down, the innumerable lines of wear upon the metal casting up flickering darts into the cool afternoon shadows against the white walls.

The guard was supposed to make sure the solenoid didn't die in their care. The *other* guard apparently didn't care, and would rather see the solenoid dead, perhaps from his wounds. The solenoid was determined to die. The guard was, perhaps, outvoted.

"Why, are you regretful?" the solenoid asked, cannily, with a curious look up at them. He grinned, a bit: a flash of white teeth. Then gone.

"Would you want me to be?" the guard asked.

The solenoid looked down. "I don't know. Perhaps. It would be…fulfilling, to think that my death made someone regretful."

The guard reached for the tray. They picked it up, stepped out of the open doorway, placed it on the cart. Closed the door. Locked it with a click.

Their shift was over.

~

They walked back home. On the road in front of Elly's place a child was sitting with a broken stick, one of the group that had been playing yesterday. The two ends where the stick had been were wrenched apart, and the guard saw that it had broken as though it were a green stick; jagged and thready, and there was green in it still, brightly, and the sticky drops of sap. The child was holding the halves of the stick, one in either hand, and pressing small fingers to the broken ends as though in confusion, just staring down. The stick had been a strong stick, straight and well formed, with cool smooth bark, and here it was broken and weeping as though it had the water to spare. It was a sight so ordinary—and yet so *strange*—a solemn child with a broken stick in two hands—that the guard could only stare for a long moment, and there were questions they hadn't even thought of suddenly crowding at their lips. Why was it broken, where had it come from? Around this tableau, the whole city went by unknowing, unnoticing, as though nothing at all had happened. Bicycles swerved past and cars honked and carts were pushed and people called and yelled and sang and radios blasted and the wind shrieked and the sun shone. And then Elly swung open the door, the bell ringing *ting-ting!* and said, "Something the matter?"

The guard blinked, turning as though pulled, shaken from something uncanny where the only rule had been to step close, still, closer, needing to ask the child *why*—"No," they said, dumbly. "Nothing." And walked inside into the cool shadows of the familiar little space and felt like the whole world had zipped shut behind them like a tunnel, so quickly thrown back into the ordinary that they almost tripped, dizzy with it and cold, out of the heat of the sun.

When they turned back to look, the child had gone.

They ordered a sandwich and sat down in their place by the window. A few feet away, behind the scraped-up counter, Elly cut the sandwich in half with a sharp knife. *Click-thum.* It caught the light of the bell or the door that opened at the same moment as a customer walked inside, a tired-faced someone with hands in pockets. Elly paused, glancing at the door, and the guard took in the whole scene: the knife which had flashed out some sort of gleaming prism onto the bare wall, and half across the ceiling: a rainbow, blued. The way the air was filled with the noise and dusty wind that sank back as the seal thudded shut, as the door jangled back into place. So quickly that the moment was past, the customer was at the counter and the light was gone, but from where the guard sat with their hands around the coffee mug the light from the window just touched the corners of their knuckles and the dull bare wall still seemed to show the afterimage from the knife, and the guard was struck with a sense that they had sat and watched a moment that would not come again, and one they should have interacted with, somehow. But they had not.

Elly took the order, and the customer wandered over to the other table, and then Elly came by with the sandwich that had been cut. She smiled, catching the guard's eye. "Rough night?" she said.

"Sometimes I think—" the guard said. They stopped, then, because they didn't know what was supposed to come after, or if there had been anything. They took a long, bitter sip and put the mug down onto the table, stained with rings, the unfinished wood, and soft with use. They were struck with the sudden urge to ask about the knife. "Do you—"

It was just a kitchen knife, the guard knew, and the power of that glancing sunlight had nothing to do with polished steel, and in truth they had never talked with Elly about anything personal, though they had known her for years, so that to suddenly say *were you also aware of the uncanny thing that just happened,* would be not only inappropriate but completely deranged—so that by the time the guard had said "do you" they had reconsidered the urge that had pushed them to speak in the first place. They fell silent with a quiet, shameful relief, because it was easier not to risk the—

The—something.

Elly walked over to the other customer and the guard realized the song that they had been composing, which they had been hearing, constantly, in the air around them since they had found the spark of it—in every muted click and thunk, in the murmur of conversation, in the songs and the static and the cars and the wind, had all fallen silent.

They could not recapture the thread. Even the noise of their spoon against the mug's surface—*clink,* was merely one discordant tone without cohesion. *Clink. Clink. Clink.*

They found themselves suddenly unhungry, and took the sandwich to be wrapped at the counter, and glanced toward the back of the store in vain for the knife, as though it would be sitting there still. Then they walked home, up the steps and into their room, putting the wrapped sandwich into a cooler under the bed and then tugging their shoes off. It was a bright, warm day, and yet they could not make themself climb out the roof hatch to the open sky, they felt so unmoored and adrift. But instead, they lay back on their bed, closed their eyes, and quickly fell into an uneasy slumber.

They had the dream again. It was the complex, but more broken down now than ever. Crumbled walls, and the locks on the doors had long since rusted. Each open window chased with hardy vines, the roots, thin brown crawlers racing up the endless white. The other two prisoners were gone, and the guard didn't think to wonder at it, walking through the empty corridor to the last door. There, curled up on his side, the solenoid dozed. The blood from his wound had stained his bandages and seeped into the prison-issue fabric of his loose clothes. It was quiet, very quiet, except for the *whif-hhahf* of his breath in and out, in and out, in and out. The guard sat down across from him, rested one hand hooked through their belt. There was something so unutterably forgotten about it, as though the solenoid was truly the only living creature left for miles, or more than that. And, turning, somehow: through a window, or a gap in the cracked walls that the guard had not noticed before, they saw that it was so: the whole city was in ruins, not the ruins of destruction but of abandonment, parched and pained, with the high shriek of wind rasping its way over the cracked puzzle of the earth.

By evening, when they returned to work, the sound that had overtaken all remnants of their song was just a continual beat: *thump-thud, thump-thud, thump thud.* They rolled the cart down the corridor, went in to feed the feral one, which was curled up in a pitiful corner and snapped at them halfheartedly when they got close, and the one who wouldn't speak, and then the door at the end, where the solenoid was.

They took the bowl in their hands, remembering the way the solenoid had tipped it, yesterday, remembering its shape and how it had been so solid, and yet existed far beyond the limits of its shell; now it was merely one of many identical bowls filled with swill, and when the guard stepped inside, they saw the solenoid dozing, sheltered under his bright electric wings.

"Hey solenoid," the guard said, quiet, as though afraid to disturb; and remembered, suddenly, the dream. Just as in the dream, the wound on the solenoid's leg had bled through. The guard put the bowl down in front of him, and bent to carefully touch the solenoid's shoulder. Then those eyes opened, staring up at him, but the solenoid did not speak.

The skin was dry, the eyes sunken, and the guard realized suddenly what the sound had been that they had heard since they'd woken: it was the too-fast, racing gallop of the solenoid's heartbeat, which they felt under their fingers now, taking the solenoid's palm in their hand, pressing their fingers to the wrist.

"You won't change your mind, then," the guard said, gesturing to the bowl.

Slowly, as if with difficulty, the solenoid answered. "No. I'm… sorry."

The guard sat down beside him. The door of the cell was open onto the long bare hall, and their shift was over, and yet they stayed. They stayed until the sun had really come up and fell burning through the lone window, and the solenoid's wings fluffed a little, feeling the warm touch that had pressed through the carefully-built boundaries of the complex. The same light danced forward, skated across the edge of the bowl as though in dizzying circles, vital.

By noon they could hear the other guard begin his rounds, and a shriek went up from the feral one's cell. The solenoid hardly flinched, so deep was he in a fitful dream, and the guard began to hum tunelessly, *Lully, lulley, lully, lulley.*

He bare hym vp, he bare hym down, he bare hym in to an orchard brown. Lully, lulley, lully, lulley.

Many years ago, they could recall, their mother had sung the song; an old tune and old words. It was not the song that they had been composing, but it was the only thing that would appear, now. They watched the rise and fall of the solenoid's breath, the knotted tension of his shoulders, and wished suddenly that he would open his eyes again. But he did not.

And, by nightfall, the solenoid was dead.

They closed the cell carefully behind them, locking it with their ring of keys, and pushed the cart through the hall and into the storeroom, and locked the storeroom doors. They changed out of their uniform into other clothes, walked out of the complex onto broken asphalt and a brilliant spill of stars; stepped onto part-deserted streets, past the gleaming that broke, like occasional shimmers, through the iron-wrought gates in the walls, behind which the night people congregated.

Down a side street a door was open, and a crowd spilled out into the cobbled alley; they passed on the main road, and stopped, looking toward the sight.

"You know, sometimes," someone was saying to the person next to them; all in silhouette; the long, slim cord of an earbud hanging from one ear and a tinny noise of some unidentifiable music playing, drowned out by the noise of the crowd. "Sometimes I think we don't ask the right questions. Like sometimes asking the right questions can fix—"

The guard, stopped in their tracks, stared into the packed, crowded place in the noise and the light. And this person half-dancing to music no one else could hear was talking with a hand on another's arm, eyes shadowed and glittering.

The war was over. It had been over for years, now, and our side had won, although no one was sure, anymore, what that entailed, or what we should be celebrating. And, eventually, the guard pressed forward, walking by rote along the crumbled streets through the city's dark, past the CLOSED sign swinging behind the deli's glass door, and even further: past the corner that led to the guard's house on the right, past street after street, all of them, straight or crooked, thoroughfares and alleys, leading on in endless succession. The night was still and open, and the roads led east, and each footstep was another small noise drifting, music-less. And the wanderer hooked their fingers into their belt, just as alone.

* *The Falcon Carol that the guard sings is a medieval song whose original writer is unknown. One interpretation of the carol's imagery is that it depicts the Fisher King from the Arthurian Holy Grail tradition.*

⁂

A Universe Akilter

i.

"But you don't love me."

"What do you mean?"

"If you loved me, you ought to have greeted me with 'Miss Soli what a wonderful—take note of that word, *wonderful*—evening it is' instead of a simple 'hello.' One can greet any acquaintance with a mere 'hello.' It is almost as bad as ignoring one altogether."

"I don't think that can be the case," I tried to protest, but unfortunately the lady had already decided on her feelings and nothing would change them.

"I think you want me dead," she proclaimed, in a loud, quavering voice; and all around her the ballpoint-pen eyes of her associates elongated toward us in mawkish interest. Behind feathers and fans, I could hear the trumpet-loud belch of gossip approaching. With every train-whistle shriek of the lady's tirade—here is something like it, as far as I can recall:

Degenerate! Oh! Despicable! And not even washed your shoes! What reason did you have for leaving me that evening last June, when we were at the train station, waiting for the mail? Did the mail even arrive? No! Not a bit! I have found certain letters in your own hand—oh yes, I've found them. Do you want to see?

Not letting a moment of my protest daunt her, she procured them: from out of her long furred parasol; reams and reams of the stuff all in brown ink, sludge-brown and beetled, as lame as an orange half-digested. "Explain. This."

The utter silence was as curious and uncertain as a spider's laugh, and quite as tenacious.

"I cannot," I said, seeing the evidence before me. I stammered. "I cannot."

"You see, you have treated me wrongfully. Take the damn things. Take them all!" She pushed them into my hands. Piled and dripping with the smell of overseas ash and heavy. They fell out of my paralyzed fingers, tracing circles around my shoes, which had been muddied from the rain last evening. On the way back from the opera, Miss Soli had been in such fine spirits—it had been a flash of something brilliant in her that captivated me; and I can recall wondering if the hard times between us were over at last.

Still the papers were a complete mystery to me, for I had not written them. Yet it was without a doubt in my own hand, with my own name at the bottom, signing, dear, my love, little darling—to a lover I had never had!

The laughter began roiling. On every side, roiling, and the righteous fury of lady Soli made her face as red as a radiator painted red.

"Don't! Not one word!" She turned to her fellows. "He says not one word in his defense! Have you ever seen such a reprobate? I feel wounded, utterly wounded—" her great black lashes clumped together as she blinked; her face shimmered with fat, blobby tears. They dotted the papers at my feet. They seemed to have enough force that I was not surprised when I gathered up the entire handful and edged out the door, because the salt of her tears repelled my hydrophobic spirit. But it was raining outside.

The porch, a midden of a thing, stopped nothing. From the brim of my hat, the rainwater laughed at me, slipping over the words in my hand. I stuck everything in the pockets of my greatcoat until they were bulging open and I felt ill—sick and ill! The back of my throat was sour and scratched with sweetness. I walked out to catch a cab, and the mud slopped over my shoes. The laces were caked in mud. The sky was caked in a grime of smog and rain, stuck and cracked to the earth. By the time I had managed to pay the requisite amount, I was shivering, and I did not stop even as the heating turned up and great gusts of dry air blew into my eyes.

ii.

When one has just had a most public and humiliating rupture between one's mistress and oneself—for reasons of a person of no existence—there is really nothing for it but to become familiarized with the crime. So having taken my things from our shared rooms to a hotel on the other part of town, I set all the letters upon the bed and tabletops and half-draped over the frowning face of the mini-fridge, and as they dried, timorously, I took off my coat and puddled it in a heap on the floor. I took off my shoes, and my socks which were grimed up to my ankles in an unpleasant arc, and my shirt, and my trousers, and my smallclothes, and my hat. Until at last, wearing nothing, I went into the bathroom to take a shower and found that the water was cold. Colder than the rain in fact, and so, staring into it, my spirit quailed. I couldn't do it: step into that icy stream. It was more than I could bear. Instead I wrapped myself in a towel, still sweating and shivering and unclean, and returned to the relative emptiness of the hotel room.

The blinds were half open. The chicken-colored light smeared its way through the fog-stained glass. My toes shuddered on the miserable carpet. I had not eaten anything but hors d'ouvres at the gathering. I had been planning to make up for my lack of breakfast and lunch with lady Walstone's famed dinner. But now my stomach rebuked me.

I sorted through the letters by date in order to read of the affair I had had.

iii.

It started last summer, or rather at that time when spring is ending and summer has just opened its arms in welcome. I can recall that at the time, Miss Soli and I were staying at the Hotel Rip. It was when her interest in cello had just begun to fade, I recalled, and the music that had filled our speech became laced with silence. Still the air had been bountiful and I had never seen bluer skies. Every day, if one cycled down the path, one could look over a small stretch of white sand dunes into a glittering expanse, and there were crowds of tourists at every corner—ourselves part of the throng of that unwilling designation.

> Little Sky, I saw you—I do not know who you are—standing on the edge of that small beach, pulling the sand with your toes. Your dress was chequered, blue as a print in a print shop. I would have tagged it a falsity but the sky behind you was exactly the same, as though in reproach. All morning I sat here, watching the dark feathered curl of your hair and creating bets as to the color of your eyes—I was quite partial to green, and had

> already composed sonnets in their honor, when you turned my way and I saw that they were brown. But the soft chocolate depths of them, with the barest glint of light when the sun caught the edges of that tilting moment between warm iris and the deep void of pupil, cast a tea-colored spark. I was entranced by the subtlety in those eyes, those ordinary eyes, and I decided I would write to you. There is no way you will ever read this, of course, for I will not send it, I will not get up and hand it to you—something so forward from a stranger—but merely remember your image, here, and this moment in which I saw something beyond perfection and imperfection.

Just as I read this, I recalled everything that I had written, but I knew that I had buried the letter in the sand, never to be found. Yet in its strange, formless, inexplicable way, I knew that she had answered me and written back, in a universe slightly akilter to this one.

I wished fervently that in some way I could read her letters as well, this nameless shameless girl, who led a different me to start my next letter in such a manner:

> You impudent creature. Of course we can never really understand anything from merely observing. Did I not just say that you were nothing but a figment? And a figment you would have remained, in my life, if you had not answered me as you did. You see? Now I must add to my basket of attributes about you: foul-tongue, sweet-breath, too-clever mind. You asked me what I would say

to my description? You are right, right in every particular. I am obscene and vulgar, and I walked down to the beach in shoes. Actually I did not walk, I cycled, and thus the shoes. I didn't know how I would be drawn onto that shifting uncertain surface until faced with it, that soft granular blanket in which sinking is the only thing that can ever be done. Without a moment's thought, I stepped out as though I could float, but my shoes slipped, and ungainly, like a stick insect, I remembered my body. I remembered the limitations of all built things, and how shoes are meant for flat surfaces. Yet my pride had been set into a flame and I did not feel able to so easily take off my shoes. You might add to *dangerous eccentric* 'a complete fool who overthinks the slightest things' but perhaps you are already aware of this defect in my character.

My face, of course, is angular, and that is something I have had to live with. With a face like this, I could become either an artist or an investment banker. Every other opportunity is really a non-option.

But I think we were talking about you, my love—

What is the reason for that sidelong tunnel? For what reason did you plant lollipops in the sand? Do you ever get tired of building castles when the waves continually uproot you? Do not look for poetry in my reply, for I'm nothing but straightforward: the seaweed in your blouse disturbed me. It was worse than the mice listening to the band around the corner, which I saw you glance so disdainfully toward. If you are oil, then—?

This other version of me, whom I will henceforth refer to as *the fool,* was already leaping headlong into a tête-à-tête with our mysterious lover. Yet myself, I had picked up my pens, stuck my hands back into my pockets, and walked back up the long slope. I had picked up my bicycle and begun skimming over the snap-pea clatter of cobbles taking me ever further from this mysterious *her.* I did not know what I was missing. I had no pang of regret in my heart, I did not glance back even once at that late-noonday sun and the black sharp shadows. The trees above whispered unfathomably, the red riots in them crowing, the marble top lawns falsely shimmering. Then there was a light and I had to wait at the curb. The sweat on my skin dried as the wind of that rushing force paused, as I, the cyclist, was demoted to pedestrian, waiting in the heat, to be beset by flies. I waved my hand sharply and someone on the other corner glared at me, as though I had been gesturing rudely. The cool refreshment of water lay behind me in the ocean, the soft shadows of a bed in the villa, and in the town was the possibility for ratiocination. Ugh! What a bore, all of it (I had thought) full of my own artful ennui.

I should have done any one of those things, but instead I rolled into town and bought a newspaper, and cured my spirit's malaise by depressing it with knowledge of the world's spiraling futility.

iv.

> This afternoon went to a funeral procession through town. There was much merriment and a few scattered flowers that had already gone rancid under our footsteps. After that, the ballet was a relief, though it was un-

gainly, with the heavy reverberations of their pounding steps, the wide sunwheel tulle skirts opening above those snaking legs. Your own amusements sound much more pleasant, all in all, and I do hope I shall one day be able to join you at the museum. I saw your drawing, lines growing softer in oscillations from the point of your utensil, as the folds of grit rubbed off into shadow upon shadow, and darkened my thumbs.

What a performance you have made of my face; putting some heavy strange mystery into the eyes that never existed. But we do that to each other, of course, being merely each others' figments. Oh little Sky, what secrets have you threaded into the wrinkles of my jacket's turned-up collar? What message are you sending to yourself the long way round? Is it narcissism after all, or is that only my reflection distracting me?

If I had your talent with charcoal I would add another, and that would be the birdsong angle of your wrist, reaching to tie the ribbon on your shoes. I only saw it once, and it was not such a pretty picture then, for your shoulders were sun-peeling and red and you had a tired annoyance in your rust-dust eyes as you tugged at the string. Away from the here and now, in memory, it becomes one of Degas' ballerinas, something unselfconscious and echoingly real. But I know you have never danced, and I would not want you to. As I said before, there is such a heaviness to those movements, a falsity that is uncanny. Perhaps only we, with our careful manipulations, can pretend we are being as honest as it is possible to be.

Please, look in the mirror of your wash-bowl, chased with bluebells. Watch the dripping curls of your own dark hair, and find a picture within it, one that I would draw, if I could.

Such went the missive, and I could taste the lightness of that previous summer, though the drizzle had grown colder outside the single stale room. The bed was flat and pressed down, where I lay piled upon squelching towels. Alternating bands of light darted, spinning, through the low blinds, as car after car went past, lighting up the empty darkness in a somber tone, red light hollowing its way over the dip of my own angled nakedness. I shivered, and the blank ceiling was still, and the heater blew a pallid steam that barely reached my toes. Nothing but a candle remained on the table, and the papers, crumpled and drying, tossed with the scent of travel.

However did I fall from such a whimsical height, I wondered. In that nothing-matters-mood, everything was sensible, and there was no such thing as the slow, creeping embarrassment of my situation. If only I had truly written these things. Perhaps the me-that-had was now sitting somewhere else, safe under a blue sky.

V.

The butterfly's axial orb disturbs me.

Having spent now one full afternoon watching its frantic flutter back and forth from the spurn-tree, while S—— talked incessantly about her friends and the pallid unfortunate descriptions of the recent soirée, I have come to realize this. There is just something so darting and purposeful, and yet without admitting of the fact. Furthermore, it is full of movement, except when it is still, and hiding the colors of its wings by turns. I know you have drawn many things, and indeed the umbrellas of the café you sketched yesterday remind me of the folded wings of the butterfly; but an unreal version of it. Of course, once you put something to paper it is of necessity unreal. Nothing of the café remains in the two-toned umbrellas, just as nothing remains of the coffee and the kisses we shared brazenly as though we were there to be envied. But think on this: perhaps even the butterfly I watch is as unreal as my mind's interpretation of the fact. Perhaps, under the sorbet sky and the soft sharp pinch of new shoes we are all, really, staring into space, seeing just what condenses best into our previous understanding, bisected occasionally by something resembling the truth, and which consequently scares us so much we turn right around and thenceforth avoid it.

I do understand what you mean about Galatea. The question remains—am I Pygmalion or Acis? Those two tales do have rather different *drifts* (and perhaps the life of a river spirit is no bad life after all, though one must be killed to do it—still, that does seem rather more *your* style. Which leads to my other potential: you are Galatea, sea-nymph, in spirit; moonlighting as Galatea the beloved crafted from stone. Which one would you rather associate with? (I have told you my preference, so we are fair). Of course there is still a certain self-focused arrogance to the casting. If drawing is more akin to carving, etcetera…

> This is what I pondered during the endless luncheon; that is, when the butterfly let me rest, and that was only for fleeting moments. It darted this way and that way behind S——'s head in reproach, a mirror to my wandering thoughts, and consequently drew my attention to the fallen garters from the washing line that had lain itself over the blueberries.

What a strange difference I found, looking back at a version of myself that had never once existed, except indeterminately. For when I had watched the selfsame butterfly I had only felt the crushing weight of the minutes and an uncomfortable daydream about flinging the chocolate sauce into Miss Soli's face. Yet here went the fool on a lengthy tangent about mythology, likening his lover to the sea. If in fact she was the sea, I wondered at his recklessness in diving toward the waves, wondered, in fact, how it was that we had diverged in such a crucial respect: that *he* made mention, even in jest, of reinventing himself as a river spirit to join her.

It was a hard irony that seemed particularly pointed, what with the stiffened papers still damp along the edges, and the incessant rain outside my roaring door. With one hand upon the pile that had begun to form as I sorted the missives by date, I glared outside at the soddenness and the muck and the cold. It is one thing to be enamoured of the sea on a fine summer's day and another to be drowned in icewater.

I left the papers behind for a time, got up and began fiddling with the disdainful coffee maker, shoving the packet open and spilling what hardly resembled ground beans so much as strong-smelling dust and waiting for the water to boil. The machine churned and stopped, churned and stopped, boiling at the slowest pace and wheezing in between as though finding the whole situation above its meagre abilities, and myself beneath its notice. Then when at last the coffee appeared, it was scalding and torturously tasteless, even filled with ripped packets of cream that I turned into novelty wastebuckets for the pet cricket I had never owned.

vi.

Smog. A blend of smoke and fog—a "fog" created of atmospheric pollutants. Something that crept slowly down the sodden streets and rose like an uncomfortably strong ocean. Inside the room, the gas-lamps' wavering reflections did nothing for the uncertain yellow that pieced itself under the door and filled the entire space with a thick and tepid claustrophobia.

I took a sip of scalding coffee and regarded the room. In this saturated night, with the candle burned low, it was nothing more than an orbit, a cubit or a qubit of indeterminate size and shape. The dank paper smelled of mildew and soot; the windows were streaks behind the blinds, the bed, with its surfeit of pillows, was nothing but a galley moving ponderously through the dark. I had tried to avoid the sea, but the sea lapped in through the figmented, pigmented cracks between door and window, layered in air. I was still hungry, though the strong stench of the coffee that filled the room did something to assuage it. It was growing warmer, at least, and with a blanket thrown over my shoulder I absently picked up the next letter I had written, perusing it between sips of coffee that grew steadily cooler as my body warmed, the simple act of heat-transference one that reminded me of the impossibility of thinking one untouched by the world.

Interesting.

Dear little Sky, you always compel me to another perspective, yanking me backward from the precipice of the pool. As you say, there is no reason why both cannot be true; and indeed there may be some duality to all nature and all story. For if it were not for the binary sequence we would be stuck in place, and without two things to combine there would be no variations (shades in pigments; you see, I do know something about art.)

Actually I *do* know something about art; if only about the particulates of it. I, too, know of cochineal red, and the boiling of bugs preserved as something other than themselves, I know of snails and the royal purple stink. If colors come from mineral or biology, the answer is the same, each must be boiled down, must be unmade, to create something new; whether we ourselves were first living, or only breathed to life the moment brush was put to paper or waxed wood.

It's a heavy subject matter, I know. I meant to talk of light things: sorbet, and linen, and décolletage. But when I think of light, now, even that turns the direction of my thoughts only toward the nature of uncertainty, of the movement of waves and the individuality of particulates. In this system of both, I dreamt of the sea.

I dreamt on the veranda, in the sun, under an umbrella, and the surf came crashing into my dreams with the grace of a rude elephant, or an errant ballerina.

> The lancets and lances went charging through the ordered predictability of my mind, and I woke up under a shadow, for the sun had gone during the course of my sleep, and the air was pregnant with rain.
>
> I do fear for the future. Which of us does otherwise? Many times I have a way of ignoring it, and then it slides past me into the present, which will as soon become the past, and so I don't let it alarm me. But sometimes, and only when I am talking with you, I wonder. If, indeed, this holiday ends—and it will…if, indeed summer ends and turns over, as it always does, to the sadly ponderous autumn, then will our minds, which will be full of different air, and our skin, which will be new, and even our brains, which will continue to keep time along with the electrical mechanisms of our ambiguous insides, so careful and messy all at once—if, in fact, time goes on, will you remember this fondly?
>
> I don't ask if you will remember me. That will happen, or it will not, as the world wills. I ask if you will remember *this:* this careful fearlessness, this wild hope. Keep it, if it suits you. It if is inappropriate to wear, among whatever society you find yourself in next, then tuck it near your breast as a favour, and consider it a gift beyond any words I might manage.

He truly was a fool, then; Love's Fool. But the novelty had worn off, and something of the general hopelessness of existence had impressed itself upon him. Caked in melodrama, as usual, but he bared his sadly beating heart to the whims of the Capricious. There was an honesty on this page that almost unseated me, this something which had started as a lark, a sweet whim, an indiscretion to while away a deciduous summer. The other me, the Fool, had with every continuous word traveled further from the usual tracks of my own thoughts, until now it was less like looking into a wash-house mirror than a fun-house, and wondering at the strange distortions it implied. Like waves, certain parts expanded and contracted with each movement, until the head and all the limbs went jumbling together into a merry jig and lost all coherence, all semblance of the selfhood I prided myself on.

For the mind, which had opened itself to the sea, had begun to change its shape, as a coast does. Such a bewildering transformation had occurred in a universe akilter, while I meanwhile had dreamt of walking slowly to work in the morning, and finding that I had forgotten my hat.

vii.

My love,

There is always endless confusion, and endless irony. You, who now exist, will turn eventually into myth, or fade into obscurity. I say this not to be harsh but merely as a reminder of the capriciousness of fate. Even if you were to be renowned as the greatest painter of the age, like Zeuxis and Parrhasios, and could lure any passing viewer into your trompe-l'œil, the walls would fall eventually, and the paints and their pigments with it. But don't think I brag that your monument shall be my gentle verse; for the truth of the matter is we are neither of us famous. (Don't take my words to heart. Many

> times it goes the other way; perhaps I shall travel the paths of the future only as your strange muse, all my words forgotten in favor of your oil.)
>
> I suspect it's not the hope you were looking for. On a personal level, I find your art more than "charming;" it is wild and unaccountable, just as all art should be. Therefore put aside the words of your critic. What fools one will never fool another; and like the holographic photo at my aunt's house, which shows its illusion only from one point, the effect depends upon what mind the painting is framed in—and each brings her own.

Locked in the stillborn gloom, I pressed at the edges of the water-stained paper with my fingers and thumbs until it crackled like the snap of ice. The mug was empty; only a soft stain remained. As I placed the letter down, and drew the blanket more firmly around my shoulders, I considered the Fool's words. He was right, of course, about the fluidity of meaning. Furthermore, some may place secrets within their works, while others will stumble through just happy to have placed a few sentences into a coherent context, only to find that others have created an entire latticework of secret meaning. But, surely, I wondered, interpretability only goes so far. To go further would be to strike out onto one's own adventure, breaking the mass of the art's finished illusion. Truly, unless one wished to have utter control over the end-point and the meaning of the personal existence which was the work, and therefore denied it out of base fear, one would have to admit that piece inspires piece until what is left is a continual work of references made, understood and misunderstood, used and misused, bartered and stolen, written and rewritten and transformed; and that the work—all work—is a mutable thing, created by many, influenced by time and place.

viii.

A certain friend of Miss Soli's greatly disturbs me. It is not in the tubular protrusions of her jowls, nor yet the flounces of her Viennese skirts. It is not in her gait, which is ordinary, or her topic of choice, which tends to the banal, nor even her manner, which is as nondescript as to be almost insulting. It is, perhaps, something in her eyes—which have a certain way of judging—and perhaps also in the conversational turns she makes. You are, say, talking about the perennials, and quite soon you are suddenly realizing that this friend not only disparages any opinion you may have had on the subject, but doubts you have the perspicacity to come up with an honest opinion anyhow. If one really has no knowledge of perennials, it is only worse.

And nothing is more unnerving than having to see that individual at a garden party.

Perhaps it is in the very ordinariness of it all. For instance: if a tsunami were to suddenly pillage the coast, that would be a tragedy, no one would deny it. When gases of poison reach incrementally through the air, killing everything in its path, we all understand a wrong has been done, although we may have disagreements on the why or the how, or even the who. But the curious apathy, mixed with boredom, of the friend of Miss Soli's—that is truly terrifying. For it is the size of a great whale, and it hovers galomptuously under the surface of the grass and inside the flowerbeds and under the embroidered parasols, chased with marigolds, like slugs.

In the fact of such, one really wishes for a be-hatting—for all the hats to go flying away of their own volition into the air. Thus, in the face of absurdity, we could laugh; because it is the world in microcosm, but blown to a manageable proportion. But the miniscule vestments in which existence tends to travel is of a much greater impact, though small in scale. For you cannot quite pinpoint either the why, the where, the who, the how, or even, and most distressingly, the *what.*

A friend of a friend of Miss Soli's once threw a glass platter like a discus and it concussed an unfortunate gentleman with some force. It is still the talk of gossip today. But no one gossips about the way three cups were misaligned, and one without water; or how when a child was tucked into bed the blanket was forgotten, or the strange tenor of a hoarse voice trying to sing backward. And when I had finished visiting with twenty or thirty acquaintances of Miss Soli's and found myself unaccountably ill-at-ease with the entire apparatus, the entire machinery of existence, all turned inside-out and upside-down, I could not blame the parfait or the luncheon at four thirty-seven, or the choice of entertainment at the harpsichord or the fact that L——, a noted rival of mine in the business of plays, was in attendance. For there was nothing whatsoever to complain about. And yet—

Listen to me, I have still not gotten over it. The broken stem of a flower, and two small stones that fell

> down into my shoe. The undulating sea-serpent hiding under the grass, which is really no serpent at all. It would be presumptuous to call it existence, and more presumptuous to call it nature, and folly to call it society. What is it, then?
>
> Is that, perhaps, what gives it the uncanny aspect? That it has no name?

This missive was just as I expected, although in my reality I had spoken of it to no one. I began to wonder, in fact, if this alternate version of events was really a sunnier plane, or merely the same one put through contortions. For if, even in the kindest mirror, all blemishes are still accounted for, then why should anyone wish to be on one side or another? True, the Fool had his Sky—I also had a sky, and one that was invading my room even now with its yellow-sea grit. I had called it a flight of fancy; yet the mire had followed, as soon as the floodgates were opened to truth, and the Fool opened his mouth to a creature kin enough to listen.

ix.

> I am in similar difficulties. The title, at least, is quite clear to me—"Down in the Sungrove Garden." At first I thought it would be about a small child, later I had fanciful images of straight-backed trunks going up to disk-like trees, and imagined it an orchard, where the lead would go during certain moments in and around instances of the confusion and depravity of the rest of the play. But when I sat down to write it, the only thing

I came up with was this fragmentary dialogue.

"Down in the Sungrove Garden"

B: I want you to think of someplace that makes you feel safe. Someplace warm, secret, quiet—a place you can just exist.

A: Something endless.

B: Is it?

A: Like a möbius strip. Endless and self-referential. It exists on its own.

B: Does anything exist on its own?

A: Of course not. But for the sake of the exercise…

B: Of course. I'm going to count down from ten, and when I get to one you'll be there.

A: Down in the sungrove garden.

B: Exactly.

A: The disks are made of yellow gold. Very soft; when I touch it with my fingernails and press hard I can trace my own outlines into the causeway. No, it's on a wall of course; an arch, a mural. Every time I see it I recreate it like an architect looking at ruins. I might create the fluidity of dolphins from a few crumbled pigments of rainbow…

B: And around you?

A: Yes, the trees. Each limb intertwined until I'm under a bower through which the light shines. It's very soft; I hear birds and rustling animals. It's all very perfect, very surreal. There's nothing to disturb the image my mind has created. No buzzing flies or centipedes. No mud or sweat-sticky skin. It is almost like being in a museum, the way the temperature is always perfect—and we are in such silence. And, of course, the art made out of every unplanned piece. The cast of sun on the grass that reaches up to my elbows. It's an illusion of course; almost like one of those holographic pictures at my aunt's house. It only looks good from one point. But from that point, it lights up the way no painting could ever hope to recapture. I stare at it for hours but gain no insight. All I have is a memory I can turn into a string of words. An inadequate description, incapable of creating meaning between the bridge of our minds. Have you ever thought about the gulf?

B: Constantly.

A: And you don't find it depressing?

B: I spend my time working, and remind myself that existentialism is as meaningless as any other human invention.

A: Very clever! I doubt it works.

B: No, but I turn my phone off every night and don't check the news more than necessary.

A: There's a river there.

B: What does it mean?

A: I haven't the faintest. It sparkles like everything else; ripples each one over the other.

Moving and never changing, changing and never the same.

B: Have you stepped into it?

A: And ruin my shoes? Of course not. No, I jest—but the truth is, if I step into the river once, *will* I be the same when I step out.

B: Or will it.

A: I knew we'd end up talking philosophy.

B: This is your mind. Your garden.

A: Perhaps. Sometimes I doubt it. Sometimes I doubt its perfection. And yet every time I retreat here I can believe that I'll be okay. I can curl up on this concrete path, warmed by the sun, and stare through the patterned branches of the trees, and the green and gold and bronzish red of their leaves, and like the afternoons of my childhood time extends…

B: Why do you believe you'll be okay?

A: Because I'm here, of course.

B: And at other times?

A: I have to contend with the world, which is, as we've established, not half so obliging. It's selfish and terrifying … I don't mean to insult existence. I really don't. But there's only so much I can *take* at once, so I filter my truth slantwise through the limbs of the trees.

B: Everyone does.

A: And some are convinced there *is* no truth. Perhaps they have a point, but it's not exactly a solid foundation upon which to base action. I'm an optimist, you know. Assume there's hope and act accordingly, and you may find yourself having succeeded. But if you think nothing is possible you'll never try, and will spend your life in anger and misery to boot.

B: And does that fix anything?

A: Not a bit. Why else would I need this garden?

B: It sounds lovely.

A: I'd take you there, if I could.

B: If such a thing were possible.

A: If you touch the palm of your hand very gently and brush your fingers across it, that strange uncanny feeling is exactly what I'm trying to convey.

B: Uncanny? And yet your garden is perfect.

A: And perfection is uncanny. Or do you disagree? I'm not saying I don't believe in the illusion, but if I took you there, I'd suddenly realize how much you're not the thing I made you out to be. I'd start to think of how we never meet outside of this, and how I don't know where you come from—or, conversely, how long you'll remain in this world. Like all my other acquaintances, one day I may wake up to find you gone—dead, perhaps, or merely vanished, and I've never quite found the Zen I need not to be terrified of that outcome.

B: You need to take more exercise.

A: Stop the thinking. Bridge the mind-body gap.

B: Even that's an illusion, there's only body.

A: Please; that's an even more terrifying prospect. But I understand. I overthink. It's something that happens when I talk to you; you oblige me.

B: Do you overthink, or do you merely spit out worn references, cobbled together with scotch tape?

A: I didn't know we were talking about originality. I never claimed to have any.

. . .

The chief problem of which—I'm sure you can see quite plain—it will not entertain the masses, while for the avant-garde it will only seem trite. I retreated into self-reflexivity in order to stop the critique before it appeared (for then I can say, if one were to accuse it of being bland and monotonous, "that's the point"—)—but that is not the point, and we both know it.

Now you know. If this makes you feel any better about your own work, my dear, tell me, for this rubbish seems good for nothing else; it shall certainly never see the light of day. And yet I have to write *something,* or the world will think I am really nothing but a dilettante. (If I am, then that is a private matter.)

These letters were becoming less and less amusing to me as I read. And now, finding my own failure of a half-finished work thrown back in my face—"Down in the Sungrove Garden" being the only play I'd managed to continue last summer, in between the increasingly ill-advised jaunts with Miss Soli and the ever-more-frequent trips to the café to brood—it was nothing but a mockery. I had consoled myself for some time, during those languorous afternoons, when I drifted about the summer-house peering through gauzy curtains, that if the play fell through I still had Miss Soli, and that if the ardour between ourselves had cooled I at least still had her patronage. It was really for that reason that I had not broken things off at once, and—in a tryingly convoluted manner—the same reason I had not been able to write. For I consoled myself the other way as well, based upon whim—that if Miss Soli were to tire of me, as it seemed likely she would, I would have, at least, a new masterpiece to unveil to the public. Instead, I had nothing but a collection of love-letters which could not even be salvaged as a poetic device and published as a bunch.

Yes, I considered it—pulling together these water-stained pieces of another life and trying to pass them off as my own genius. But it was worse than pointless. For not only did they lack titillation, they contained too much of my own maudlin thoughts, and to place them out for a penny for the public to look over would be a worse embarrassment than having to read them myself. In fact, I did not *have* to read them, and yet something compelled me to peruse the stack, some interest in what had changed and what was still running parallel, some morbid preoccupation with the Fool's existence.

But I needed a break. I put the paper down, pulled my blanket even further about my shoulders, and went poking around the dingy room. There was an ice-box, sans ice; there was, of course, the bathroom with its cold water, and a great profusion of novelty soaps, there was the mirror which showed a wavering reflection, a pinched and tired face which seemed neither to have eaten nor slept. There was no miracle hiding among the folded towels or the rolls of toilet paper or the small tube of toothpaste. I turned on the water, again, hoping futilely that it would have warmed; but it was still nothing but ice minute after minute. I turned it back off, and watched the condensation drip down the tile.

There were no slippers, and my feet were cold.

I wandered back into the other room, closing the door.

I once read a book—I don't remember the name—in which a woman did nothing but lie on the floor and consider making tea. It was a contrived set-piece, for a book, though as a play it would have been a tour-de-force. At the time I had chuckled at how contrived it was. For what would cause humanity, which of its own nature thronged together, to separate into pieces—and how long would such isolation really last?

All of a sudden I was struck with the knowledge that I needed to leave this claustrophobic room. And yet there would be no leaving while the air was still as thick as soup and as unbreathable. I was stuck here for the near future, and I had not even thought to bring a book, or entertainment, or even a few stolen éclairs. This severance from the world I had so derided was now foisted upon me.

With nothing else to turn to, I went again to the letters, and picked up the next.

x.

Little darling,

I saw the first unarguable evidence of autumn today in the cut-back lavender. Every morning, when I strolled down the garden pathway to the village, it would entice me with its heady fragrance and bright purple profusion. Now those bending stems are gone, and the whole way seems emptier and more bare. There is something in the light, also, which has changed. I'm sure this was no surprise to you; you must have noticed much earlier than I, a holed-up creature, what with the way you dip your paintbrush into light in every piece you make.

I kept your last sketch, and—as you insisted it was only a scribble and folded it up yourself—have kept it in my wallet. This I looked at, today, when I ate alone, as though by paying homage to you in such a way I would increase your chances of success at the gallery. You will have to tell me what happened when you return.

I see something in your rendering I have never seen before—a sadness. Oh Sky, if I could take your sadness from you I would, though it makes for brilliant art. The shadows under the charcoal vase were deep, and the crumpled napkin, which lay underneath it, became a mountain range. I saw the corner of my own hand, somewhat blurred behind the glass.

There is never enough suffering, as far as the world is concerned, and we invent more on a whim; I wish that whomever invented yours would find that they always have only crumpled napkins wherever they are, and lukewarm water. It's a paltry curse, as far as curses go, but if even once it makes you smile, I will consider it a complete success.

xi.

There was some irony in the Fool's curse. Indeed, I thought it not beyond the pale to imagine that it was *he* who had caused both this continual wet gloom and the fact that the water ran nothing but ice. In fact, I may have exclaimed an audible "hah" upon reading that last letter, and it was with some resentment that I put it down and looked about the strewn bedclothes. But I found that, to my great surprise, in my engrossed perusal of the Fool's journey, I had missed the fact that the pile of letters yet to read had grown slimmer and slimmer, and now, with the placing of this last one upon the careful, rippled stack, there was nothing else left.

But this was impossible! I still had no clue, yet, how the affair with the young Sky had ended, or if she'd gotten into the gallery as she should; in some way I had assumed that these letters would have followed the entire loop of my past, leading up to when I'd had them shoved so unceremoniously into my hand last night, amid the peering circle of gossipful watchers. To find the missives cut off so abruptly—and with neither explanation nor apology for the fact—disturbed me greatly.

It was with combined distress and resentment that I got up and paced the room, first in a whirl of thoughts, and then merely to move, though there was nowhere I could go as of yet. The candle was now only a stub, and the darkness was nearly complete, except for the light that muddily threw itself between the blinds.

In the corner, upon the desk, stood a pile of empty creamers, like a rubble of stones or a great and miniature ruins.

There was no sense in an end like this. Worse than the senselessness, there was no satisfaction in it, even of an unpleasant sort. There was just an empty gap.

But there was nothing that could be done. What had been written had been written on a different path, in a life not quite my own; and it was done with, for whatever reason. This I tried to tell myself, as I paced with ever more frustration upon the mealy carpet. I began to shiver, for the chill was real, and I'd left my blanket lying on the bed.

I cursed the Fool, and the Fool's curse on me—and I cursed his ever-present inability to finish what he'd started, even in a bunch of letters chronicling a love-affair.

It seemed a sorry state indeed to be so cursed by a self that didn't even exist.

I paused by the window—the air was still thick and soft and entire against the pane, so that it was nearly impossible to make out any detail beyond the wavering light. And at once the surety came upon me that if nothing else I would—if nothing else I *must*—break the Fool's curse.

With this sudden purpose—I went into the bathroom, and checked again—the water was still cold. I stared down at the unrevealing porcelain as the few tremoring droplets swirled down the drain.

Another way needed to be found.

So I put myself to the task. If the water would not heat itself, *I* would heat it.

I went back into the bedroom, filled the small coffeemaker with water, and stuck my empty mug underneath, plugging the whole contraption in. It boiled, in slow fits and starts, and then wheezed the water out in a great jumble of complaint.

The small mug in my hand was scalding hot, the water steaming and smelling still strongly of cheap coffee. I brought it into the bathroom, threw a towel into the tub and poured the water onto the towel, then filled the coffeemaker once again and stuck the mug underneath.

This I repeated, for at least ten repetitions, waiting with no small impatience in between, until the towel in the bathroom was soaked completely through. Finally, I stepped into the tub and picked up the sodden cloth, wrapping it around me. It quieted my shivers at once. I closed my eyes, feeling the water drip itself over my stomach, down my legs, pool itself at my feet; I brought the towel over my neck and scrubbed it across my hair, I covered my face with brilliant warmth and an odd coffee-esque perfume.

Then, the tiredness that I had not felt before descended upon me with sudden force.

I left the towel in the bathroom, dried myself with another, and returned quickly to the other room. I placed the letters upon the table and crawled under the covers, tucking them up to my chin. I therewith closed my eyes.

xii.

My dream came upon me as all dreams do: without beginning. I was wandering through the street-corner on a June evening, and beyond the low hunch of the station the shrieks of trains went by at convoluted intervals. Miss Soli was beside me, holding a feathered fan of an ostrich in one hand, and it moved the slow, hot air only slightly, providing momentary respite against the continual heat. We were soon to return; the holiday was over, and there was a careworn inevitability to every movement.

"Do stand still, would you?" she complained. "You're giving me conniptions."

I obliged, and leaned against the brick, but that didn't help, for in another moment—

"and now you are tapping your feet. Why, what is this great impatience of yours? We're only waiting for the mail, it's hardly an excursion."

"I'm only—"

"I know, I know," Miss Soli sighed ponderously. "Your artistic temperament. It hates stagnation. You're too flighty to be held down. Something of the sort, yes?"

" . . . yes. Something of the sort."

"Mm-hm." She sighed again. "Why, I do believe the train is late. Can you imagine? And by nearly half an hour! Oh, there's the station-master—perhaps he'll know what the issue is." She strode off in regal fashion, bearing down on the station-master with the full force of her intensity, and saying in a clear, clipped voice, "My dear *sir*—"

I took the first opportunity to slip away. Down past one geometric corner, where the dry grass was hiding, and over a low stone wall. I suddenly found myself behind the whole contraption, in that empty nothing-land which has not been prettied up. Following the posterior of the station for some time along the bare, windowless back wall, further than seemed plausible considering its small size from the front, I finally turned a sudden corner and found myself on the brink of the city.

The pyracantha were in a riot to the left, reddish berries bowing down with jeweled, smoky precision, and I knew there would be no passage in that direction, the thorns were too great. To the right, there she was, waiting at the appointed spot, as she had not been last time. I recalled her hastily-sent note:

> Didn't get in. It's really a hopeless endeavor, I fear; this art of mine. I wanted to meet once more but the train comes early, and I have to go back to my family once it arrives. You know I have valued our little fling, far beyond what, I think, it has ever mattered to you. You believed in me continually, and I never knew how much it was *that* that lightened my steps enough to soar like the sky you named me.

She turned around, then, in surprise as I approached. "Oh!" she said, and a soft smile graced her features. "I didn't think you'd arrive. It takes far longer to drive from the villa, and the times don't line up any way I make my calculation—"

"In dreams, all things are possible," I said portentously, and she raised her eyebrow in my direction. I grinned in awkward amusement.

"You sound like a coffee-mug," Sky said matter-of-factly.

"Yes, it's just because I've had it on me," I explained. "The smell lingers."

"I see," she said, and leaned forward to discover if that was indeed the case. (It was, and we spend a few delightful moments taking the time to taste a sweeter indulgence; with a few swirling kisses pressed from tongue to tongue.)

Finally, it was she who leaned back, with a rueful sigh. "I

didn't regret our parting, but I regretted never having this last conversation, you know," she admitted. "I still do; I go over it constantly in my lonely moments, imagining what you would have said if you were really here."

"I know," I said.

She reached down to pull a stocking that had begun to slip. It only sagged further, and with a distracted scowl, she plopped herself onto the dusty ground, hiking her skirts to her knees in order to tie the ribbon round it more securely.

Despite the humor of the situation, she seemed far older than I had recalled, in an indefinable way I could not express. It had nothing to do with her beauty; which was, as always, artless and sun-bronzed. It may have been her clothing, which was sensible travel stuff I had never before seen her wear. It might, also, have been the way that, when she tilted her head back and closed her eyes, a great weariness seemed to fall upon her.

Without another word, I sat beside her on that curb against the brick, that continual city stretching on before us into a haze of mist, the tangle of bushes separating us from the small town where we had met. There was a sense of endless expanse on every side but our own, and yet no way to get there.

On a sudden thought, I reached into the pocket of my coat—as thick and heavy as a winter coat, even in this heat—and pulled out the stack of yellowed papers, which I had read and sorted; the letters I had sent to her. "I noticed you lost these. You're welcome to keep them—that is," I stammered, suddenly blushing, "if you want to."

She opened her eyes, then, and smiled again. Leaning forward, she took the papers and pressed them to her heart for one moment. "Thank you," she said. "I had another drawing to give you, as well, but I left it outside of the dream. I'm sorry."

"It doesn't matter," I assured her. "It was you I wanted to see, anyhow;" I said, and I brushed the fingers of one hand through her frizzed curls, and rested it against her cheek. Her solemn mahogany eyes, deep and reflective as an obsidian mirror, fluttered in and out of sight under the line of her lashes.

At last she said, "I was thinking, about what I told you once; of Galatea. I said I might as well be both, and I said it flippantly, but the thought has been turning over in my mind these past months. Sometimes when I move my arms under the cool afternoon shadow of a mausoleum, I feel everything like Galatea crafted from stone, and I know then that the inevitability of our parting was always fated. Other times, when the light shimmers against the glass, or I see the stream of water into a bowl filled with dandelions, and I place my hands inside against the grit, I know that I am instead a nymph, and that I will do anything to keep you with me. I am both. But not only that—for when I recognize your face in the drawings I make, I know indeed that I am Pygmalion, creator of what seems most beautiful to me, finding through the lines I place what was already there in the paper's emptiness. Other times, when my sadness is great, I know that I am Acis the lost, and it is you who transformed me into a creature of the waves. I am both, and I am all.

"And," she continued, at last, slower, and her eyes traced their way across me as her lips spoke; "once I had realized that I came to recognize another thing. If I am all—so are you."

"That seems," I said at last, in a voice very wavering, and quiet, and deep, "exactly fitting."

xiii.

I awoke with the disorienting feeling that I had traveled a great distance; I recalled my dream with perfect clarity. Because I knew how these things faded without proper attention paid to them, I did not get up immediately, but caught, first, the precise reflection of Sky's brown eyes in my mind, and the dusty place in between and beyond the rest of the world. Once I had that, I cast my thought over every part of the dream I could recall, starting from the train station and my wandering off, and went through the whole thing, paying close attention to every color, every building and unimaginable vista, every word spoken, not once, not twice, but three times entirely, until I was convinced it was as firmly in my memory as it was going to get.

At that point I allowed myself to take stock of my surroundings. The half-closed blinds let in a cheerful afternoon light, and the smog had finally lifted, leaving the air feeling clearer, lighter; as though a pall had gone from my very lungs. Even in this dry and stuffy room I could feel the difference.

All the detritus of last night was still laying about —my coat, in a sad heap on the floor, my clothes hung over the mini-fridge; the indubitable coffee-maker. And beside me on the table, right where I had left them, were the letters that had been given to me. I got up, re-dressed in my clothes from yesterday, which were still as grimy and unpleasant as ever, though at least they had almost dried in the night, now being only vaguely damp. I tidied up the room as best I could, and then picked up the letters in order to fold them and place them into the pockets of my greatcoat. But it was to my great surprise that, when I saw the topmost sheet, I knew quite at once that it was a letter I had not read before. A new one! And not written in my own hand, but Sky's. *Unimaginable!*

Eagerly, I sat down to read.

Dear one,

You have always found me fearless. And I have never contradicted you on the matter, because something about your assumption of me was bolstering. You caught sight of me on the beach one day, on an afternoon where I walked disconsolately down to the ocean to find solace, for everything in my papers, and everything I drew in charcoal, recriminated me.

I did make fun of you, then, for you cut such a funny figure, ungainly wading through the sand in your shoes and your buttoned coat, looking as though you'd been waylaid en route to some great party. But I made fun of you out of admiration, and I think you know that. At least, you smiled at me as if you did—not with the condescending turn I am all-too familiar with, but with something captivated. I saw you, glancing at me from the corner of your eye, while we both played coy and pretended not to notice the other's gaze. I saw you take a sheet from your pocket and scribble something down, fold it carefully and place it with great ceremony into the sand, almost buried. I saw the sly mischievousness as you did so, and I recognized the invitation there.

Do you know, I almost turned away, then?

In a universe akilter, I might have—might have

turned back and fled down the beach; pretended my afternoon had never been uprooted by such an event as it had been. I very well could have, and in fact I knew it—everything in me urged me to walk away, out of fear.

So when I say you have always found me fearless, I suppose I mean that you have found in me a fearlessness that comes and goes, like the tide. It was at a low ebb when we met. Even the bright sun did nothing to assuage my worries; even the knowledge that I had a whole summer here with nothing to do but tutor a sweet-tempered child in the mornings, giving her lessons in maths—

Well, you know all that, of course. I think you may have even seen her, once or twice, when we met outside the beautiful blue-and-white house, with its picturesque gables and its delicate lace curtains. She was very enamoured of you, in the abstract; for she knew full well we were involved in something full of mystery and intrigue, and would always sigh over the romance of it.

Ah, youth! 'Tis a funny thing. But I felt the same.

You made me feel the same.

It is for that reason that I feel as though I've done a great disservice to my own soul in avoiding you today, as though depriving us of a goodbye was anything akin to a kindness. It was cowardice, plain and simple, and I think I was aware of the fact even as I fled.

Now, without the rosy light of dawn and the fine sand of the beach, without the walks through the park every afternoon—will you recognize in me that weakness, and still see me the same?

> I suppose it doesn't matter if you do or not, for we aren't to meet again; yet I wanted you to know. From where I write this at my desk, lamp turned low, in the depth and stillness of night, I find my mind chasing the memories of this past summer as though I might be able to grasp a thread within the shifting sand, something that I can sling this letter across. Perhaps it might reach you, then. Wherever you are.

I folded the letter, when I had read it, and placed it on the stack. I tucked the stack carefully into my pocket, turned around once more to survey the room, making sure I had not left anything behind—and then, with a strange lightness in my step, at odds with the preoccupation invading my thoughts—I left.

xiv.

The city was already bustling, for I'd slept in late. I took myself over, first, to Miss Soli's apartment, where I began to pack everything of mine as well as I could; it fit easily into a carpetbag. I left her the key she'd given to me when we started our affair, on the counter where she'd not miss it. And then I made my way back to other lodgings, staying for a time with a few old friends of mine in what amounted to a gabled attic. Though it was small and drafty, it was rich in cheer, and continually filled with music and talk late into the night; always with one visitor or another and plenty of food that seemed to turn up in dribs and drabs, brought along by the innumerable visitors.

From this place, I took stock of my life, and bodies of work, of which they were all, unequivocally, a mess. "Down in the Sungrove Garden" was unsalvageable. Of other pieces in progress, I had some sketchy beginning of an operetta involving a haunted house and the adventures of a few siblings; a monologue about a small, inlaid box that was far too scattered to be any use to anyone, and a monograph upon the subject of perennials, which I had no desire to continue at all—a pity, for it was really the only one of the four that was of any quality.

And of course, there remained the letters between myself and my mysterious Sky.

I had thought the letter I found from her might be the last, but to my great interest, that was not the case; there were still a handful left, each one appearing at odd moments, always laying on top of the stack that remained. They did not come with any regularity; I recalled that she'd had many obligations that left her little time for anything but a few sketches here and there, and her letters—the memory became clearer as I read, and recalled those that had come before, that I had once had the pleasure of laying hands on not in this universe but another—had always been less frequent than my own.

The very next one from her started, in fact, in this way:

Dearest,

I took up drawing again, which I haven't since June. Oh, no reason—I know you'll ask and I plan to get ahead of you this time—merely busy, I suppose; and if you really want to know the truth, my inspiration has been flagging terribly since the incident last summer. I know, I know—you'll tell me not to despair, and I do remind myself of it continually.

You may be aware—I had the feeling you were, though we never talked of it—but I did have a small success once. I was quite adept with watercolours of gardens, rivers, everyone having a wonderful time, you know, a real body of female work—and it was met with some acclaim. I still get mentions of it, now and again. My oils and everything else—the more realistically treated subjects—less so, and that is where my heart is taking me these days. Sometimes I sit down, telling myself sternly just to knock out a few peaceful images of what I'm already known for and it's just a *terrible* tragedy, how stilted they become. I am afraid I've always been a slave to inspiration. I do envy you, really; writing is so much easier—you can cross out words you don't like while I can only erase so much before the whole paper is worn through.

I like to imagine that when we parted—as if to balance out my own sad lack of progress—you've really finished one of those plays you always complained to me about. I think about you selling every copy in the run within five days. I know! A silly fantasy, but it does give me some pleasure. I am sure that the truth is much more mundane, but—I hope—still pleasant.

To that end, I write to you as though to a friend, for I know that even if we are no longer lovers you will always hold a particular space in my heart, us two being alike. If I've timed the dream right, if I've thrown this into the river at the spot where I should have—well, then you'll get this letter, and if you do, I'll know.

Don't ask me how! But I am somehow convinced I will.

XV.

My sweet,

I am incredibly happy that you got my letter. It gives me more joy than you can think of, to know that this strange contrivance of mine has actually worked. And don't feel bad for not writing back; it's a one-way sort of thing, and there's a lot of maths to be worked out in it, which you've told me yourself you can't follow. I shall just imagine your responses, and if I get it wrong ninety percent of the time, well, I shall be content in never knowing!

It was the strangest thing, but I found myself pondering your play—the one you sent to me—in the letters from you that I lost, somehow, in the confusion of boarding the train. I remember much of it, and I even think I have the beginnings of an idea on how it might continue—though I have the feeling that I will not have worked it out before this parallelism between our universes comes undone again, and I am no longer able to send these to you. Because of that—because I know there's not much time left—I sat down, during a free moment this afternoon, and really thought to myself what it was I wanted to say—what I would *absolutely* want to say to you if this was the last time we might speak. And, do you know, I was so delighted to realize that I think I've told you everything—

By which I mean, though it saddens me that this will soon be over, I am convinced you understand the most important things.

There is nothing, perhaps, that I really wish to *say* to you with such urgency, but I do have one last regret, and that is that I can't send you my painting. It was inspired by the dream in which we met, and it won't be done in time. But I wish desperately for you to have it.

Give me just a bit longer, and—if I can send you even one more letter—I promise, I'll have figured it out.

Though it seemed unlikely, I did believe Sky's promise. Though there were weeks, now, where nothing else appeared; and I knew she was correct that the strange alignment between our universes were fading. One afternoon I went out walking, hiding under an umbrella for the drizzle was chill and increasing. The park was quite near, and I picked up the pace, hurrying with a sudden knowledge that if I was to get to the river soon enough, I might see something uncanny.

Along the way, I'm afraid, I bumped into a young woman, and had to apologize profusely. She was wearing a veiled hat, and there was something about her strangely familiar. In fact, I was just about to ask if we had by chance met before that—well—I still am not certain what happened. Perhaps I blinked; or turned my head at a sudden noise, or something of the sort; for in the next moment she had managed to walk away—somewhere down the wide street, which was empty enough that I could pick out every individual, and unless she'd gathered up her skirts and *sprinted,* well, it was rather unlikely for her to disappear so quickly.

I followed the road again and did make it to the park and the river at last; the river which was now frothing, fed by the rain. But nothing happened there; and quite soon, tired by the chill, I made my way back.

xvi.

That evening, when I opened my desk-drawer as had become habit, I saw that there was one more letter; a very small one, this, taking up a few lines only of the sheet. I knew, without even reading it, that this was all she'd been able to send through, and I knew also that there would be no more letters; we had really drifted from each other's orbits for the last time.

So it was with a certain amount of ceremony that I sat down by the desk, lit a candle, and read this message in the quiet evening, imagining her sitting at her own desk, toiling over what to say, her mouth a frown of concentration, her hair loose in her own chambers, her fingers smudged with paint and ink, as they always were under her gloves.

My Love!

I told you I would find a way round it. The painting is called "The Street Corner"— I've sent it to you in another dream; and though you might not remember the details, if you buy a pack of oils I think you'll find that it's in your fingers still, and will come forth without obstruction.

Yours always, through whatever distance,
Sky

I had no paints on me at the time, but I did as she instructed, and though I ruined a few canvases at first on trying to figure out the hang of the brushes and how to spread the stuff round, she was quite right that as soon as that was down I knew exactly what I had to create. It did come to me in a dream; though if it was a dream the night I got her last letter or another time I cannot now recall.

But that is how—in all honesty—I came up with the painting that is now the talk of the city. It was not my work at all, but another's, and I rest humbly under her, my tutor.

It has taken some thinking, this past year; for that is how long this strange interaction between us has lasted. It has taken much thinking, in fact. I have considered the Fool—and I have considered how much I am, or could have been, he. If I was not, it was of the same cowardice that Sky admitted to herself, in honesty and in private.

But I am grateful to him, this other version of myself, for pulling me along this path, for without him I would never have met Sky. And—mayhap I am also grateful to myself. For I know indeed that if I had not taken steps to break his curse, I would never have been able to find the right dream at the right time.

Perhaps that is how all life is, though. A series of steps and missteps, chance and the seizing of it. If you, dear reader, have seen the painting—take another glance. For sometimes it's the second look that matters most of all.

"The Street Corner"

The bricks are grimed behind them, and their dark coats are old; the cuff of the slightly taller figure, where it rests upon a pile of letters, is worn.

His head is tilted, and his hat obscures his expression; as her hat, with its lace-edged veil, does hers: there is the barest hint of nose and cheekbone turned up, and opened lips as though she is speaking.

There are many other figures in the painting. Pedestrians hurry by around them, carriages rattle in the distance, but in this one spot the movement seems to ease, and it is clear that both figures are fixed on each other, with a soft intensity of knowing.

It is a detailed, proportionate painting, done in shades mostly of brown and grey and dirty cream; only a few glints of blue hide in the wavering heavens, and the cobbles are chased with sludge. Still, everything shimmers from the recent rain: the dewdrops on the jackets and the umbrellas of passers-by, the shimmer of the water along the street; the few small windows, glinting like shards in the distance.

There is one puddle right below these two figures' feet, and it seems possible they are even stepping in it; the way the shadows of their boots blend into the water below them. But—and here's a secret—if you look close enough, you can just make out that the reflection in the puddle shows a clear, brilliant sky; and what seems to be the limbs of tall trees, glancing as bright as the liquid sun.

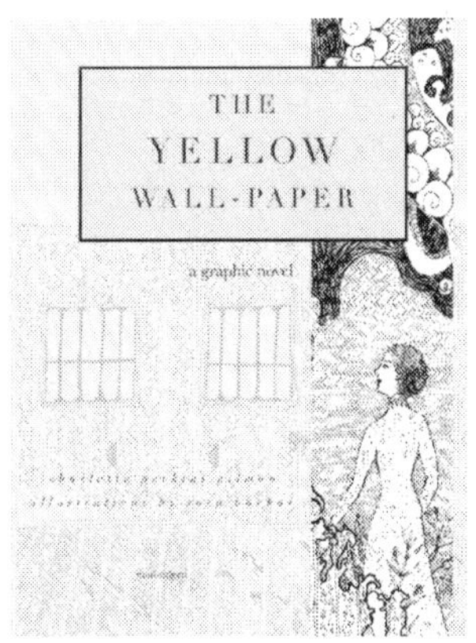

Also from T. S. Poetry Press

The Yellow Wall-Paper: A Graphic Novel—
full text by Charlotte Perkins Gilman, 1892
Illustrations by Sara Barkat, 2020

Made in the USA
Middletown, DE
02 December 2021